The
SACRED ROOTS *of*
Ofelia Rosas

The
SACRED ROOTS *of*
Ofelia Rosas

CHRISTINA MONTOYA

Book Design: mycustombookcover.com

www.authorchristinamontoya.com
Chrsitinam77@yahoo.com

Printed in the United States of America

ISBN: 978-1-7328244-0-9

First Edition

ACKNOWLEDGMENTS

To all of the special people in my life, thank you for your support in this endeavor. And thank you for freely giving me enough love to sustain me for a lifetime, I am blessed beyond measure.

With gratitude to my friend, and mentor, Dr. Frank S. Dávila. Your support of this work and your presence in my life over the years, has meant the most. I could not have completed this book without your constant encouragement, you reminded me that I can accomplish anything that I set out to do, and for that I am truly grateful.

DEDICATION

Eli, thank you for giving me a purpose in life, I'm privileged to be your mother. There are not enough words to express the magnitude of love that I have in my heart for you.

Sean, Ryan, Ricki, Aly, DJ, Eriana, Julia and Isaiah-Auntie Kiki loves you.

The children of La Paz, Honduras, I will never forget all that you gave to me.

This book is also dedicated to one of the greatest women I have ever known, whom the main character is loosely based on-sort of reimagined. Grandma, I don't think you realize how inspiring you have truly been. You are a real treasure, Angelina Villa.

In Memory Of

Dad, Grandma & Grandpo David, Linda Salas, Ruthie

TABLE OF CONTENTS

Preface

IN 2017, A NEW DECADE WAS UPON ME, I WAS TURNING 40 YEARS OLD. I decided it was time to accomplish some new goals. And so, I referred to my Bucket List to gain motivation. My Bucket List mainly consists of travel destinations, with the exception of a few miscellaneous items. On that list, I wrote that I wanted to write a book. I came to realize that I hadn't accomplished some of the more ambitious items, such as writing a book. It seemed like it was the opportune time, so I thought I should try. After all, I figured that I might actually have a few stories to share, through my travels and life experience.

A few months leading up to writing this book, I experienced small magical signs that led me to believe that I should begin this work (some of which are incorporated into the story). I received sort of a green light to begin, and so I did. I didn't realize at that time that this book would have elements of magical realism in it. I was writing a piece that was like a soft whispering voice, which caused me to dig deep within myself, to convey a message. A message I would later feel responsible to share with others. This endeavor eventually became much more than a personal goal.

Writing didn't come without some doubt; at times I felt uninspired and lacked direction, as I had never written a piece of this magnitude. Then, one day, I remembered something that was a pivotal point for me, to believe I could actually accomplish this. I recollected something that my seventh grade, teacher wrote on the back of my report card, regarding my writing, in Religion class. *"Christina is a very conscientious writer."* I never understood what she meant until I undertook the challenge of writing this conscientious book. Who would have thought that years later, everything would make sense? I am convinced that I was destined to write, and furthermore share this book with you.

Throughout the process, I was asked what I was writing about. I couldn't confidently answer because of the many interwoven topics. But now, I can certainly say that this book is about life. It's about finding moments of hope, it's about accepting true love, it's about believing in something, even if that *thing* is not real. And most importantly, it's about being a person who can have a positive impact on someone's life.

My hope is that something that you read in this book will move you, prompting even a slight change in your personal journey. The same way in which I had to be ready to write this, I hope that you will be receptive, while reading it. If you internalize the underlining messages, it may give you a renewed hope or remind you that you too have a purpose. Ultimately, my wish for each of us is that we would *"Do Something"* to change the world around us, whether it's within our families, communities or somewhere out in the world, thus forging our own remarkable legacies. I hope that you enjoy getting to know the legend that is Ofelia; so far, she is the most fascinating woman I have ever known.

To my future grandchildren, may you forever live a life filled with wonder
and adventure.

Ofelia Rosas

OFELIA ROSAS, "NANA," WAS A DAUGHTER, SISTER, WIFE, MOTH-ER, GRANDMOTHER AND A GREAT GRANDMOTHER. She was blessed with a long and prosperous life. She took her final breath at the tender age of ninety-nine. She outlived most of the people she had known throughout her younger *and* older adult years. She experienced challenges like the average person does, but she was resilient and persevered in the midst of those tough times. She and her husband, Leo, had four children, Hector, Martha, Marisol and Juanito.

She had numerous grandchildren, nineteen to be exact. She had thirty-eight great grandchildren at the time of her passing. She was highly cherished, and rightfully so. She had mastered the art of making everyone in her family feel special, in their own way; she had the capacity to love them equally. In her later years, she wasn't as keen, and often times forgot the names of some of the younger great grandchildren. Although it was a challenge to remember each of them, one thing was clear, they were all hers, every last one of them.

The stories that follow are about a handful of Ofelia's offspring.

Her sacred roots would continue to grow, even after her departure, one person and one interaction at a time, further impacting the world.

CHAPTER ONE

The Lion and His Cubs

AS LEO SAT IN HIS CAR ON TOP OF THE MOUNTAIN, WITH HIS GUN IN HAND, HE HAD FLASHBACKS OF MEMORABLE MOMENTS IN HIS LIFE.

He was forty-three years old and had spent the last twenty years working as a police officer. He had witnessed many things over the course of his twenty-year career, as most police officers do. He was originally from Colorado. Since he was young, he aspired to become a cop. Leo began his career in Colorado for a couple of years, before he applied and was accepted into the NYPD. He didn't want to move to New York and seemingly had no choice because his wife, Angelica, had to go back to care for her ill father. After months of discussion, he finally obliged, because he knew how much Angelica loved her father.

Moving to New York came with many challenges. Leo was in culture shock when they first arrived on the east coast. The contrasts between Colorado and New York were undeniable. He and Angelica first met in Colorado, at a church convention, when they were teenagers. Their parents belonged to a national ministry that held a conference in different cities every year. It was love at first sight. After meeting, they kept in touch through letters and phone calls. Leo promised he would marry Angelica when they were old enough. And just as he had promised, they married the year they both turned eighteen.

Angelica moved to Colorado and they began their lives together. They were so very different; she was of Puerto Rican descent and raised in the Bronx. She had a New York accent and her view on life was very different than Leo's. She said that growing up in New York felt like she had been raised in several countries, because of the diverse cultures that made up New York City. And even though her parents tried to keep her as sheltered as they could, she caught the train every day to attend one of the best schools in Manhattan. Daily travels to Manhattan attributed to her world view. She was very knowledgeable in ethnic foods and had friends from varied backgrounds. She certainly loved all people and valued their diverse way of life.

Leo thought Angelica was the prettiest, brightest, most genuine girl he had ever laid eyes on. She thought very highly of him as well; she thought he was a kind soul and the two of them were absolutely inseparable. He wasn't quite sure how it would work, since they were from opposite sides of the country. He was also Latino, which seemed like one of the only commonalities they shared. His roots came from deep within the southwest. Their way of life, food, the way they spoke, everything was different. Despite their differences, their love was deep, and they were determined to make the relationship work.

Their first few years in Colorado were blissful and they enjoyed settling into their new lives as husband and wife. At the beginning of their marriage, they rented out a small apartment at one of the properties owned by Leo's parents. They were genuinely happy and diligently working on their respective goals. Angelica was in college working on obtaining a degree. Meanwhile, Leo decided that college wasn't for him, and was determined to become a police officer. He took the entrance exam a few times before he got accepted into the Police Academy. He was a tall man, six feet tall, dark, with jet black hair. He was physically fit and took pride in the way that he looked. He had a strong presence about himself, he unknowingly demanded attention from others, without effort. There was something prominent about his stature.

He was the eldest child and somehow always had the older brother kind of look. He had four younger sisters, which made him a natural protector. Even his name, Leo, which was of Latin origin, meaning Lion, evoked a strong presence. He worked out every day, all day it seemed. He was a mentally and physically, strong man. He was also a distinctively fair and balanced man, which made him an ideal police candidate. Leo and Angelica were a solid couple; they both had a good head on their shoulders. He was a little more reserved than her; didn't speak much with words. Angelica certainly made up for it, she was boisterous and outgoing. Her outgoing personality was one of the things he loved about her; there was never a dull moment when she was around. She loved Leo and supported his every dream.

Leo finally began his career as a cop and she was very excited for him. However, she was not thrilled that he was required to work overnights, long hours and most holidays, as a rookie. While he was working overnight shifts, Angelica would visit Leo's grandmother, Nana Ofelia, who lived down the street from them, in the little yellow house on Sherman Street. She and Leo were very close to Nana Ofelia. Nana loved Angelica and more than approved of their relationship, she thought the world of her. Leo was the eldest grandson, and since he was a boy, his nana built him up with confidence, higher than the Rocky Mountains.

Nana told Leo, "You are just like your grandfather, a warrior, a fighter, a man of strength and dignity." "You will never let the world change you mijo, *you* will change the world."

Mijo/mija is a word of endearment that Nana Ofelia often used, when speaking to her grandchildren. Those very words and others like that stood with him, as he continued to grow into a man. He never wanted to disappoint her and could often visualize her face, anticipating him doing something good. The thought of breaking Nana's heart certainly kept him motivated to do the right things. But his move to New York did in fact break her heart, as he was the first grandchild to move away. Although Leo and Angelica would do their best to visit whenever they could, the family, including Nana, saw them less and less over the years. They began their own family and eventually seemed to have forgotten life back in Colorado. Life in the big city consumed them. It was a fast life and they were busy with work and raising their two sons. Everything was good for them, overall. They stayed in the Bronx until Angelica's father passed, and then they moved a little further upstate for quieter surroundings, in the suburbs.

"Leo, are you ok," Angelica asked.

"Yes, why?"

"Because the boys are opening their Christmas gifts and you are texting on your work phone." He was disengaged, even at a special occasion. Angelica wore a look of frustration on her face, a look she seemed to be wearing far too often nowadays.

"I'm sorry Ann, I'm waiting for some information to come in about a case I've been working on."

"I understand, but these boys need you, we all need you."

Leo finished his text message and put his phone down on the worn-out cherry wood dining table. Angelica felt alone in raising the boys. Any time she had an issue or concern, Leo would simply tell her to handle it. He didn't seem interested in the boys nor in Angelica. Work was all consuming and Angelica did her best to be patient and understanding when it came to Leo's profession. However, being the wife of a cop got more difficult for her, through the years. During his first years as a cop, he would share a lot of things with her about his experiences, but he eventually stopped sharing anything with her as time went on. He became more protective and made the boys feel like something bad might happen while they did even normal everyday activities.

Angelica often made excuses for him and tried to get the boys to understand that he dealt with a lot of dangerous people and saw a lot of ugly things on the streets. She explained that he only said certain things to protect them. Leo was assigned to a neighborhood with the highest crime rate of all the boroughs and he was a tough cop. He never wanted the streets to change the man that he was, but over time he didn't realize that it did just that. The boys preferred not to be around him and spent more time with their mother, testing her and taking advantage of her kindness. They weren't bad children, they were normal, curious teenagers. They often snuck out of suburbia, to do some exploring in the city. Angelica hated the idea of them going to Manhattan but grew tired of arguing with them every time they asked permission to go. She was protective in her own ways because she had done her fair share of exploring of the city when she was growing up.

"Boys, the world is not like it was when I was growing up; the world can be a beautiful place, but it can also be a cruel one." "Your father does not want you to experience the cruel world and would do everything in his power to protect you from it."

Their sons, Johnny and Joseph didn't deliberately intend to hurt their mother, but they craved adventure that they believed could only be found in the city. They began running off to Manhattan during the weekends and almost daily during the summer months. They were fifteen and sixteen years old. They were still kids, but they thought that they knew everything. They were growing up faster than they needed to, and their father hardly noticed because he was preoccupied with his career. Angelica saw her sons slipping away in front of her eyes and grew exhausted trying to hold them back.

Arguing amongst her and Leo about the boys, became a common theme and they started to blame one another for the boys' actions.

"If you were a better mother, the boys wouldn't be running the streets!"

"If you were around more they would have a strong manly figure in their life!"

The blaming was continuous, and it gave the boys even more of an excuse not to be home. Johnny, the older son, was more of a risk taker than Joseph. Joseph got wrapped up into his brother's trouble but only went so far. He seemed to think about consequences more than his brother. Johnny got into a lot of sticky situations, but he always seemed to be saved by something or someone from real danger. Joseph was more of a follower, he was very loyal to his older brother and never wanted to be without him, they were very close. As time passed, Johnny began hanging around some bad people. He eventually left home for good, as soon as he turned eighteen. Joseph graduated high school and went away to Boston for college.

Joseph changed a lot when Johnny left. He felt betrayed by Johnny for him leaving the way he did, without notice. Johnny contacted his mom and brother for a while after he left home, but they knew that he wasn't in a good place. They had no idea where he was living, and they eventually figured out that he was using drugs. Angelica pleaded with him to come back home and told him that she would get him the help he needed.

He said, "I'm ok, I can do it on my own."

Many nights, Angelica drove around the streets in Queens looking for Johnny. She knew some of the friends that he had there, she figured he might be in the area. Everyone she and Joseph spoke to said that they had not seen him in weeks. Angelica cried every night and Leo felt empathy for her; he attempted to comfort her the best he could.

"Angelica, this is not your fault, it isn't *our* fault." And even as he spoke those words of comfort to his wife, he somehow didn't believe them. He started to blame himself for not being a better dad and eventually the guilt overtook him. Over the next several weeks, Leo had co-workers looking for Johnny in every borough throughout New York City. There was a missing person report filed but no one could find him.

At that point, they had exhausted all efforts. Leo spent the mornings looking for his son in known areas that young homeless people occupied. After Leo got off work, at six o'clock in the morning, he would change into his civilian attire and set off to look for Johnny. He didn't want to be recognizable, so he would change into his street clothes. As he searched for his son, the same homeless people he would see on a daily basis started to look different to him. He began to think about how all of those people were someone's child. Leo struggled with the fact that his own son was living on the streets. A cop's son shouldn't be homeless and living on the street. A cop's child should be following in their father's footsteps, or something along those lines, he thought.

Leo continuously asked himself how it happened, no one knew of the torture that Leo was experiencing, not even Angelica. It was a very cold Thursday morning, almost ten degrees below zero. It was heavily snowing and there were blizzard warnings for the entire Tri-State area. Leo parked his car on 5th Street and 78th Avenue. He was going to walk for a few blocks around an area that the homeless population referred to as *Zombie Land*. It was a highly drug infested area where the homeless hung out. There were drug dealings and other crimes being committed on a daily basis around those few blocks. Even though Leo was a veteran cop, he was not very familiar with the area. As he walked about the blocks, he was surprised to see so many young people.

Leo suddenly started to experience the actual effects of homelessness. There were young women carrying backpacks, men pushing carts filled with various items. Some of the young people had scars on their faces and arms, from drug use. He had seen many things throughout his career and people rarely affected him. He didn't feel much of anything after working on the beat for so many years. And perhaps making himself numb to feeling anything was a defense mechanism that enabled him to survive the tough streets of New York City. As he walked block after block, he again thought about how each of those young people had a father, a mother; they were somebody's brother or sister. Leo was deep in thought and it felt at that very moment that the whole city, the city that never sleeps, became silent. He saw young people wandering around aimlessly. Some were high, some seemed to suffer from mental illnesses, and others were just plain lost.

He regained his senses, and again was in extreme denial at the fact that his own son could be somewhere in that land of the lost. Leo saw a young slender man, with long brown hair. He was covered in facial tattoos and was wearing a brown beanie cap. Leo thought the young man looked familiar. He approached the man when he realized that he had seen Johnny with him once.

"Have you seen Johnny?"

"Who are you?" the man grudgingly asked.

"I'm Johnny's father."

The man quickly said, "I don't know anyone named Johnny," with a smirk on his dirty face.

Leo felt his anger quickly arise, he knew better than most when someone was lying. He swiftly grabbed the collar of the dirty jacket that the man was wearing.

Leo pulled the man close to him and said, "You and I both know that you know my son, don't play with me!" The man was taken aback by Leo's swift actions. His eyes grew larger than they had previously been. It was clear to Leo that the man was under the influence of some drug.

The man said, "Let me go!" "I don't know you and I don't know no Johnny!" Leo eased up on the man and with a firm finger pointed at his face, he said, "I'll be back every day until I find my son, and every day I'll make sure you know that I'm here." The man saw the badge that Leo had on his belt under his t-shirt. "Oh man, this guys a cop!" he nervously yelled.

A group of young people heard him, and everyone ran from the block. Leo wasn't acting as a cop that day but as a parent looking for his son. He knew that he couldn't act as a cop and this wasn't a typical case. He knew that abusing his authority could get him in trouble, but he was so frustrated and distraught, that he started to care less about his job and more about his son. Leo started back to his car and drove around for a while hoping to find Johnny. He had no such luck that day. The following day, Leo went back to the same neighborhood at the same time. But that morning there seemed to be less people hanging out. He looked around for a moment and saw a woman sitting on the curb, weeping; she looked out of place. She was a middle-class woman, blond hair, wearing clothes that looked like they had been purchased from Macy's on West 34th Street. Leo approached her to inquire if she was alright. He thought that perhaps she had been robbed. "Excuse me ma'am, is everything ok?" Leo asked.

The woman was startled by him. She looked up and sadly responded, "I'm alright, I'm just looking for someone."

Leo sat next to her, curious about her situation. Could she also be looking for her son, he wondered. Before Leo could ask her any other questions, the woman began to tell Leo that she was looking for her daughter. She had a picture of her in her hands and said, "My twenty-year-old daughter Chelsea hasn't been home in days." She proceeded to tell Leo all about her daughter and about how she comes from a good home.

"She just wants to live on the streets and there's not much more I can do about it." She went on to explain that she had begged Chelsea to come back home for over a year, that she and her husband were moving away to Florida soon. "This is my last attempt to get my daughter to come with us; I have left notes at every shelter in the city asking Chelsea to call home," she explained.

Leo felt helpless in attempting to help the woman and also felt helpless in his own situation. He didn't know what he could say to comfort the distraught woman. All he could think of at that moment was what his nana had always told him. He could suddenly hear the sweet voice of Nana telling him, "We never give up hope on our loved ones, we need to grasp on to the hope that the love we have given will be strong enough to guide those lost souls back where they belong." Leo was lost for words, but he somehow conjured up enough breath to speak the exact words of Nana. The woman began to weep even more at the words that he spoke and somehow, she felt like someone had finally given her an ounce of hope that eased her soul, if even for a moment. The woman hugged Leo and thanked him for listening and for his words, as she drove off in her white BMW that was parked across the street.

That morning, Leo left struggling to believe the very words that he had spoken to the woman. The only thing he could never doubt, despite life's challenges, was the words of Nana. He somehow believed Nana's every word, she spoke the truth, and her words brought comfort and encouragement. She really made him believe something good could come out of even the toughest situation. And that morning, he left feeling that maybe those words were really meant for him. Perhaps the only way he could accept the words was to verbalize them and in turn the words would somehow be internalized.

He thought about the conversation as he drove home. He thought about how challenging it was to be hopeful in a world that seems to be so hopeless at times; if there was anything that could help to calm his soul it was the wisdom Nana instilled in him. He seemed to be having an inner struggle with himself and the guilt he carried for failing his own son. He thought if he was home more as Johnny was growing up, this might not have happened. He thought if he was a better dad, this might not be happening. He thought if he wasn't so selfish in his career that this might not be happening. He thought if he didn't allow the job to change him that this wouldn't be happening. He thought about other parents and wondered if they had the same feelings of failing their children.

Leo arrived home and Joseph was there visiting from college, during winter break. Joseph was aware of the situation, but Leo didn't want him to see his struggle. He refused to speak about Johnny and acted like everything was normal. He acted as though it didn't matter much if he found Johnny or not. "Dad, any luck finding Johnny?" Joseph asked. Joseph was becoming a very clean-cut young man. He had jet black hair that he combed to the side, not one hair out of place. His eyes always had dark circles and his teeth were straight and his smile infectious. But that day he wasn't smiling, in fact he hadn't smiled in what seemed to be forever, not around his dad anyway. Leo gazed over at Joseph and just shook his head, *no*, in response. Joseph looked down and walked over to the table for dinner. He tucked his semi smile into another dimension and his mother wondered if she would ever see him smile again. Angelica made a traditional Puerto Rican dinner that night, arroz con gandules, it was Joseph's favorite dish. Everyone was silent over dinner and for a moment, Joseph was filled with regret that he came home for break.

When he was away at school he could be someone different, he could be Joseph. He could be free from his father's critical glare; Joseph was happy while away at school. Even though he worried about Johnny, he had somewhat given up on him. Moreover, he knew that his brother could bring nothing good to his life. He was determined to be someone great, not a disappointment, like his brother. He felt the little bit of love he had left for Johnny slipping away day by day. He thought that if he forgot about Johnny, he wouldn't feel any sorrow in losing his best friend. He was also reminded of his brother when he returned home, it was the reason he didn't come home as often as he could have. And as he ate his food, he looked up to see the photos of he and Johnny sitting on top of the mantel. He was once again reminded that a part of his soul was somewhere out there, alone.

Leo saw Joseph staring at the photos and in a sudden rage, Leo threw all the photos on the floor. As the glass from the frames fell to the floor, he had flashbacks of when the boys were small. He remembered holding them in his arms for the first time and walking them to school most mornings after the graveyard shift. He held the boys' hands tight, like a man would. Their tiny hands in his rough hands, he intended to protect them from the cruel world. Leo realized at that moment that he really did love his sons. He thought about how he could have shown them more love but didn't know how. As the boys were growing, he thought that he could never be too soft, because that wasn't how real men taught their sons to be men. Did he have it all wrong their entire lives? Should he have been gentle, and shown more love?

Angelica screamed, "Leo, what are you doing!" She frantically began to pick up the broken frames, glass was everywhere. Joseph looked on passed his parents and ran up to his room. He had no words for his father's outburst. Leo helped his wife pick up the glass. As they were cleaning up, the silence between them was unlike anything they had ever experienced. In the deepest darkest voice Angelica had ever heard, her husband told her, "We no longer have two sons."

Angelica screamed at Leo hysterically, "You don't mean that Leo, you don't mean that!" Leo left the room and Angelica sat on the floor weeping, until her tears dried up like fall

leaves in October. That night the phone rang at three o'clock in the morning. Leo quickly turned over to the nightstand and answered the call.

"This is Detective Patterson; do you know Johnny Ramos?" the man asked.

Leo quickly responded "*Yes*, I am his father."

"I'm sorry to tell you this Mr. Ramos, but we think we have your son's body, a young man was found overdosed in Queens." "We need you to come down and identify the body."

Leo said, "I understand, I'll be there in thirty minutes."

Leo hung the phone up and got dressed as fast as he could. Angelica asked him what was going on, but he didn't have the heart to tell her exactly what the detective said. He simply said, "The cops think they found Johnny." He grabbed his keys and quickly ran down the stairs. Joseph heard the commotion and followed him out to the car. Leo told him, "You're not going anywhere with me!" Joseph could sense that his worst fears were becoming a reality, he just felt it. Leo started the car and sped off; as he sped off he looked at the rear-view mirror and saw Joseph running toward the car. Leo abruptly slammed on the breaks and then turned around and motioned Joseph to get in.

The ride to Queens seemed to take longer than ever before. Leo could feel every patch of ice that was on the streets with high intensity. He couldn't get to his son fast enough. The car almost slid off the road a couple of times because he was driving recklessly. Joseph was so frightened at the way his dad was driving, as if they were on a high- speed chase but didn't dare say anything. Leo looked over at his son during the drive and could see that he was frightened. Joseph looked like a scared little boy. His big brown eyes were opened wide and he was moving his hands by opening and closing them, making a tight fist repeatedly. Leo noticed a single tear flowing from his son's eye. Without saying a word, Leo firmly grabbed Joseph's shoulder, in attempt to calm him down. Joseph quickly wiped his single tear and soon they arrived at the address that the detective provided.

Leo quickly parked the car and ran out leaving Joseph way behind. Joseph never thought he would see the day that his dad would be able to outrun him. It was a house in Queens, on Pearl Avenue. The house was abandoned and in terrible condition. There was flashing lights and yellow tape from one end of the block to the other. Leo flashed his badge to the officers that were standing on the other side of the tape, as he ran underneath. Joseph finally caught up to his dad and as he tried to break through the yellow tape, the officers prevented him from entering.

"This is a crime scene," one of the officers said.

Joseph tried to force himself in.

"My brother is in there, asshole!" he yelled.

One of the officers grabbed Joseph and pushed him to the street. As Joseph fell he felt his head hit the ice, and as he tried to get up, he could feel blood rushing down the right side of his face. He stayed there for a minute, trying to regain his composure.

As Leo ran into the abandoned house, the lead detective greeted him at the crown molded doorway. Leo explained to him that he was also an officer. Leo knew that he was going to experience a parent's worst nightmare. At that moment, he mentally prepared himself. The detective led Leo over to a crumbling fireplace where a body was lying on the ground. There was a fire going and the sparks from the flames seemed to illuminate the body. Leo visually scanned the body and moved towards the head to get a clearer view. Leo took a deep breath as he saw the face of his baby boy. There was a needle stuck in his right arm. Leo knew better than to touch the body for preservation of the investigation. He slowly closed his eyes and said nothing.

The detective asked, "Mr. Ramos, is this your son?"

Leo still had no words.

"Mr. Ramos, can you positively identify the body as your son Johnny Ramos?"

Leo reluctantly responded, *yes*, this is my son Johnny."

After he responded, all other words that were spoken by the detective became silent.

A few minutes later, Leo came back to the harsh reality of what had occurred. He remembered that Joseph was outside, and he ran out to be with him. Leo never needed anyone as much as he did in that moment. He didn't feel strong enough to comfort Joseph but rather needed Joseph to comfort him. As he ran to the street, he saw Joseph getting up from the cold ice, blood dripping from the side of his face. As Joseph saw his dad, he knew that Johnny was gone; he held his dad tightly that night and his dad allowed him to. A single night had never felt so cold, red and blue lights flooded the street, the blood from a brother's face hit the ground ever so slowly and a father's tears flowed like a rushing river. Leo and Joseph spent a few hours at the scene and then finally returned home to break Angelica's heart.

As they drove closer to their house they could see that the porch light was on; and as they entered the driveway, there Angelica sat, wrapped in a white blanket. They could tell that she had been crying and then they realized that she must have heard about Johnny on the news. Leo was somewhat relieved that he didn't have to tell his wife himself. He could not bear the sight of a mother's heart breaking; not his wife. He finally felt what many parents felt like when he had to tell them that their own children had died. He and Joseph ran to the porch and carried Angelica like a baby, into the house.

The days following Johnny's death was a dark time, the sadness in the house was undeniable. They finally planned the services and it was a beautiful funeral. Leo attended the funeral but was not there mentally. However, he was grateful for all the love and support they received from family and friends. He just couldn't express it. He was thankful for Angelica, for being strong and for her planning the services. Leo didn't go back to work for a few weeks. He didn't want to answer questions that his coworkers might ask. He didn't want to deal with anyone, at all. Joseph went back to school a few days after the funeral and they didn't expect to see him again until summer. Joseph called Angelica regularly and she was always so excited to hear his sweet voice.

"Mom, how is dad?" he asked.

"You know your dad son, he won't talk to anyone."

That's how most conversations between them went.

"Leo are you going to eat your dinner?"

Leo just sat at the table with a blank stare. He barely ate

anymore and didn't respond to her question. He pushed his plate forward towards the middle of the dinner table and headed upstairs to the bedroom. Angelica felt helpless and would light a Virgin Mary candle and pray for him every night.

"I don't know if I'll go back to work," Leo told Angelica the following morning.

She asked why, and he told her that he was done being a cop. All she could say was, "Whatever will bring you back to me, I am behind you." The guilt that Leo carried was far too heavy. It consumed him, and he no longer felt worthy of being a father, not even to his remaining son. He avoided Joseph and felt like he had nothing to look forward to in life. The guilt he felt for not dedicating more time to his sons, and not showing more love, was immense. Regret that he didn't know how to rid himself of. He wondered if he had been home more, would Johnny have had a better example of a father. He thought about what it would be like if he had hugged Johnny and told him that he loved him more. Would that have been enough to prevent his son from looking for love in the wrong places? He wondered if he hadn't been as strict as a father, it might have saved his son. He thought about how he could ever be proud of a son that lived a life of drug addiction. He thought about so many things that he could not find resolve for; there seemed to be no end to his torturous life.

Leo went for a drive one night. Without destination, he kept driving until he ended up in the Pocono Mountains, in Pennsylvania. It was still dark when he arrived at around four o' clock in the morning. He sat in his car contemplating taking his own life. He thought maybe taking his life would be the only way to relieve him from the pain and guilt he bore. As he sat there, gun loaded, he had the fight of his life. He had never experienced such an inner battle, and frankly, he was losing. He was strong, courageous and a force in his own life as a cop, but didn't know how to win this inner-battle he was in. Did he really want to die? Did he really want to leave

Angelica alone? Did he really want to be considered a coward for taking his own life? Leo struggled with himself, as he thought about his eternal destination. He wasn't sure whether he believed in God or not anymore. But if there was a God, he ultimately knew that God would disapprove of him ending his life. And just as all those thoughts ran through his mind, Leo dozed off into sleep.

Suddenly he could see Nana cooking in her tiny kitchen. She looked healthy and had a glow about her, just as he remembered her when he was young. He hadn't seen Nana for a few years, she wasn't able to attend Johnny's funeral; she was too old and frail to make the trip to New York. They hadn't even spoken after the funeral. Leo proceeded to sit down at her table, as he was always welcomed. He could not speak, even though he wanted to hug her and feel the comfort of her loving arms like he felt when he was a young boy. Nana didn't turn around completely to greet him and he wondered why she hadn't. It was as though she expected the visit.

"Mijo, what has taken you so long to come?" she asked. He still could not speak. Nana continued cooking. Leo could smell her fresh chile and rice and could see the steam coming from the pan of handmade tamales; everything was so clear and just as he remembered. Leo wanted to tell Nana everything that he was going through, and somehow it was like she knew what he wanted to say. "You are mourning the loss of your cub." He wasn't quite sure what she meant immediately but quickly remembered that she would call him her Lion. He had no choice but to listen to what she had to say.

"Losing a cub is one of the most difficult tests for the Lion," she said. "A Lion is strong and courageous, is a protector that would kill for his cubs, but he can't always prevent his cub from wandering off into the wilderness, while he is out hunting for food to feed the family."

Leo understood nana's words and held on tight to them.

"You have another cub Leo and that cub needs you."

Leo felt saddened for a moment because he knew that he had

shunned Joseph for some time. Leo could feel his facial expression turn to pure sadness.

"You have fed your cubs, you have showed them how to survive in the wilderness and tried to protect them; you are a strong lion, Leo."

And then she turned around and he could finally see her face. He wanted so much to hug her and tell her how much he loved her. Her eyes were just as he remembered but the green in her eyes looked even more pronounced. Her eyes filled with complete compassion and genuine love. "Mijo, return home and continue teaching your cub how to survive in the wilderness, he is not yet fully grown and will have cubs of his own someday."

At that moment Leo realized just how much Joseph still needed him and that he still had time to teach him how to be a great lion. Leo understood very well what Nana meant and it's just what he needed to hear in order to gain the courage to continue on with life. He tried to stand up to hug Nana and still unable to speak, he saw her turn back to continue cooking. He felt saddened that she wasn't as excited to see him as he was to see her. It's as if she hadn't had a chance to miss him, like she saw him every day of his life and hadn't missed a thing. She knew exactly what was going on. Leo felt sorrowful for not making more effort to visit Nana, after all, she was still alive.

Leo stood up out of the old torn up chair that Nana had in her tiny kitchen. As he stood up he was awakened by the sound of the car radio.

"Happy Father's Day to all the fathers out there," the announcer said.

Leo was dazed and trying to regain his state of mind. He was in the middle of the mountains and the sun was rising. He looked over to see his gun on the passenger seat. He suddenly remembered what he was doing up there and shook his head in disappointment. He was in disbelief at the fact that he allowed himself to go that far.

He immediately started up his car and headed down the mountain. He could recollect the dream he had, almost word for word. He felt encouraged and thankful that Nana was there for him in his time of desperation, even if it was just a dream, it felt real to him. He arrived at his house a few hours later, somehow energized and feeling hopeful in his new-found courage. As he opened the door he saw Angelica in the kitchen preparing breakfast. He looked over to the left and saw Joseph sitting in the living room.

"Happy Father's Day Dad!"

Leo didn't realize that it was Father's Day, a day that he thought he would never be worthy of being recognized for, again. But with Joseph's warm greeting, he felt confident that he would once again be a great lion. A forever protector and provider to his cub.

Leo ran over to Joseph and hugged him tight and said, "I love you, my son, my cub."

Joseph was taken back by his dad's actions and felt the sincerity in his voice.

Joseph said, "I love you dad, you are a great man."

Leo took a deep breath and told Joseph, "I promise to be a great dad, son because I know that you need me." "I'm sorry for not being there enough when you were younger."

And before Leo could say anything more, Joseph placed his hand over his dad's mouth, in the most respectful way he could; he didn't want to hear any other apologies, as he had forgiven his dad. Leo saw the scar on Joseph's face from the fall the night that they lost Johnny.

Leo knew that every time they would see that scar, they would be reminded of the events of that night. Even though he could not change the past, he knew he could change the course of the present. "Son, I am so proud of you; I am proud of both of my sons." "And because I have you, this family will always have a legacy." "You are next in line to be a lion and will have cubs of your own someday; I will help you prepare for the position as best as I can."

The two of them spent the morning reminiscing about when the boys were young. They laughed, they cried, and they shared a special moment in time. And later that night, Leo saw Joseph lying asleep on the couch. And as Angelica looked on, he grabbed a blanket and then walked over to cover Joseph, just like he did when he was a young cub. Angelica now recognized the man she had married, it was a beautiful sight. Still, in the back of Leo's mind, something told him that he should go to Denver to see Nana very soon. And so, the following week he went to pay her a long, overdue visit.

CHAPTER TWO

Esperanza's Sight

ESPERANZA WAS A VERY SPECIAL YOUNG LADY, SHE WAS BORN BLIND, TO PARENTS PEDRO AND LISA. Her parents tried for several years to have a child and when she arrived, they were convinced she was a gift straight from the heavens. Pedro and Lisa loved Esperanza with all their hearts. When she was born, they quickly learned to adjust to the challenges of having a special needs child. They vowed to love the precious gift that they had been blessed with. Esperanza was undoubtedly a happy girl, and as she grew her parents discovered that she had a gift. Esperanza was musically inclined; she could naturally play the piano and sing like an angel. When people heard her sing it was hard to believe that it was coming from such a petit girl. They wondered how someone who wasn't able to see, could communicate such depth and intense emotion through music. When Lisa was expectant with Esperanza, she played and sang lullabies to the unborn baby, as she went to sleep every night. She told Esperanza that she was kissed by the angels who sang in heaven. Pedro and Lisa proudly looked on as their little angel approached the stage.

Esperanza went to public school with the other neighborhood

children. For the most part, she was very well supported. As Esperanza slowly walked into the school auditorium, wearing a white dress, her hair long and wavy, she indeed looked like an angel. The same as the angels that her mother described to her. Esperanza was ready to perform for her school talent show. It was finally her turn, her chance to showcase the natural gift she had been given. She was now in the eighth grade. Her music teacher Ms. Lawson looked on as if Esperanza was her own child. You could see the pride and excitement Ms. Lawson wore on her face. Ms. Lawson had met Esperanza two years prior and discovered something special about her. But ultimately, she had no idea just how much of an impact the young lady would have on her own life. Pedro and Lisa proudly looked on as their little angel approached the stage.

Ms. Casey Lawson was a modest woman who considered herself nothing more than a music teacher. She never aspired to be anything more, music is all that she knew. She chose to teach music because her mother was a music teacher. It's as though she felt like that was the only thing she would be good at. She herself was musically inclined and could play a few instruments; she could read notes and play by ear. She was not an emotional person by nature, she often came off a little strict and cold hearted.

She grew up in an army family, her father was a well -respected Colonel, who had high expectations of her and would accept nothing less. He never showed much love, he was rigid, and on several occasions told Casey that he wished she was a son instead of a daughter, for he longed to have a son. Therefore, Casey became accustomed to acting as a son would. She thought she had to be emotionless because she thought that it was how boys acted. She never learned how to tap in to her emotional side. When Ms. Lawson met Esperanza, she knew that teaching a blind girl was going to be a challenge. She even felt a little inconvenienced during the first year, as she had to make a few modifications to the classroom. It took Esperanza extra time to enter and exit the classroom and Ms. Lawson made sure to create a clear pathway for her.

After the first year, with minor adjustments, it seemed to be going pretty well. Ms. Lawson didn't know that Esperanza knew how to play the piano that entire first year. However, she was aware that Esperanza had the voice of an angel. When the rest of the class sang in unison, Esperanza naturally projected her voice and somehow managed to become, the lead. The last day of class during that first year, Esperanza was leaving class a little late. She attentively listened as Ms. Lawson played the piano. Esperanza wondered why the music sounded the way it did. Lifeless. She decided to go over and speak to Ms. Lawson about the music.

"May I ask what the name of the song is that you're playing?"

Ms. Lawson turned around, startled at first because she hadn't noticed that she was still in the classroom. She responded, "*Seasons.*"

Esperanza politely said, "I'm so sorry Miss but that song does not sound like seasons."

"What do you mean?" Ms. Lawson asked. She was taken aback and felt offended because it was one of the original pieces that she had written.

"I mean, it just doesn't sound like, *Seasons.*"

Esperanza began to ask Ms. Lawson what seasons felt and looked like to her.

"I guess I never really thought about it," she responded.

Esperanza said, "We live in Colorado Miss, there is plenty of inspiration in this state when it comes to the four seasons."

Esperanza further explained what she thought the seasons felt and looked like. "Winter smells like pine cones and feels like warmth," she said. She told Ms. Lawson that her parents took her to the mountains during winter break every year, since she was born. "I could smell the pine cones as we drove up the mountain." "The smell excited me because I knew that we would get to chop down our own Christmas tree and do all the other special things we did while we were up there." The explanation made sense to Ms. Lawson.

She grew more curious and asked Esperanza, "What about feeling warmth?"

"Every night my mother makes me her famous Mexican hot chocolate, I could smell the cinnamon sticks. She grinds up pieces of dark chocolate and adds it to some milk, and then she sits me by the fireplace in the condo where we stay. She covers me in a big fuzzy blanket and we sit in front of the fireplace for hours until I fall asleep in her arms. I feel safe and at home because I'm with the people that love me. That's warmth, Miss."

Ms. Lawson started to think about how Esperanza had to rely on smells, sounds, physical touch and feelings, for her mere survival. She briefly felt empathy for Esperanza, and then she caught herself and immediately said, "You had better get to your next class Esperanza, you are late."

"Have a great summer" Esperanza said, as she exited the classroom to begin her summer break. Over the next several weeks, they both thought about the conversation that had taken place.

Casey had a lot of time on her hands during the summer months. Unlike other teachers that she knew, she could actually afford to take the entire summer off. She was very active, she enjoyed hiking and being outdoors. She was single, in her late thirties and lived with her cat Mattie. Overall, she was content in her life and successful in her career. Maybe a little lonely at times and so she stayed busy, filling up her time with activities, most of which she did alone. She had friends but considered herself more of a loner. As she began any day, she played a few songs on her piano. It put her in a good mood and helped to set the tone for the day. She would brew her fancy macchiato from her Krueger coffee maker, and open the French doors in the living room, to allow the fresh air in.

One Friday morning as she sat down to play, she began to play a few original songs that she had written, when suddenly her song, *Seasons*, came to mind. As she played the song she lacked concentration as she thought about what Esperanza said about the song not sounding like, *Seasons*. Casey briefly agreed that perhaps she was right. "I'll just change the name," she said aloud. After struggling with finding a new name, she became frustrated as she thought, *what does the young lady know anyway, she was just a kid.*

That afternoon after running a few errands, she decided to go for a hike. After hiking for a few hours in the heat, she decided to take a short water break. As she found a rock to sit on, she unexpectedly tripped on a pine cone. She again was oddly reminded about the conversation she had with Esperanza. She thought about how descriptive Esperanza was about things that she had never seen. She realized that perhaps Esperanza was right, the song lacked emotion, but she didn't know how to make the song come alive, so that people who heard it would feel something.

Over the rest of the summer Casey did her usual outings. But that summer started to feel a little different. She began to reflect on her life and started to set new goals for herself. She thought about doing some things she had never done before, or things that she had put off doing. She decided that she would start attaining her goals after the summer. Soon enough school was beginning. She made a list and called it a, *Lifelong List*. She didn't necessarily believe in a *Bucket List*. Bucket Lists sounded too final and more like a death list, too negative, she thought.

The first day of school Esperanza walked into the classroom and greeted Ms. Lawson with the biggest smile, and with excitement in her voice, she asked, "How was your summer Ms. Lawson?"

She responded, "It was great."

"Did you play your song over the summer?"

Ms. Lawson was surprised that Esperanza remembered the song.

"I want to show you something after class, if it's alright," Esperanza said.

Ms. Lawson had no idea what she wanted to show her but nonetheless she agreed. After class ended, Esperanza explained that she had been working on something over the summer. She sat at the piano and started playing a very moving piece. Ms. Lawson was more than amazed at the beautiful song she heard.

"That is a beautiful piece young lady!"

Esperanza asked, "Do you like it Miss? I'm calling it Seasons of Hope." She went on to explain that she wanted to show her what *her* seasons sounded like.

"I think that is such a wonderful interpretation."

Esperanza told her about her summer and this time when she spoke, Ms. Lawson paid better attention. Maybe the young lady could really teach her something after all, and she realized in that moment that the young lady possessed wisdom way beyond her thirteen short years of life. Ms. Lawson asked Esperanza why she was so wise and mature. Esperanza explained that it was due to the time that she spent with her great grandmother, Nana Ofelia, who taught her a lot about life.

Ms. Lawson decided to share her future goals with Esperanza. The first thing she shared was that she wanted to travel and visit more countries.

Esperanza asked her, "Like where Miss?"

She replied, "Hmmm....Thailand, I would love to visit Thailand."

Esperanza asked, "Well, why don't you?"

She said it so simply and so confidently. Ms. Lawson thought that Esperanza was right, why couldn't she travel to Thailand? She had inherited a hefty amount of money from her grandparents, as she was the only grandchild. Money was not an issue and time wasn't either. Since she didn't have to pick up any extra teaching jobs during the summer, she had several weeks in which she could do some exploring. Esperanza went on to explain that she would go to Egypt.

"Egypt would be fantastic," Ms. Lawson said.

"My nana says that Egypt is full of excitement and wonder."

"Your nana must be quite the traveler."

"My nana has traveled the world," Esperanza proudly responded.

The two of them spoke for a few more minutes and then parted ways. As the school year went on, their friendship grew, and they became very close. They shared stories about places they would like to visit, and also shared their love of music; the friendship became a natural fit. Ms. Lawson began to see subtle changes in herself simply by being around Esperanza. She actually started to feel some emotion and also began to feel the liberty to express herself, unlike before. They wrote some original pieces together and the music was truly special. Every note and every song inspired by a story they shared or dream they had. The music held true meaning.

As time went on Casey began to start her, Lifelong List. Her first trip was to Thailand during winter break. Her plan was to relax on the beautiful beaches, including Paradise Beach, and to explore the food, as she loved Thai food. When she arrived in Phuket, Thailand, it was more beautiful than she could've imagined. As she continued her vacation during the week, she couldn't help but to ask herself deeper questions as she experienced various things. Questions that she imagined Esperanza would ask her about the country. Like what the city sounded like or how the food tastes. Somehow everything she did seemed to be more purposeful. Esperanza told Ms. Lawson that she didn't have to search very far for answers to life's questions, that the signs were all around. She would tell her that all she had to do was take the time to read the signs.

Casey decided to sign up for a Thai cooking class. The chef, a small native woman, explained the different dishes that they would be making. Casey looked at the food sitting on the table; the chili and spices all looked very unique. As the class began to make a traditional dish, she thought about how although the chili and spices had their own distinct flavors, they all somehow came together to create something beautiful. The dishes looked as beautiful as they tasted. Casey thought for a minute about how food was kind of like people. People are different, and by combining individual talents, a community can create something divine, she concluded. The chef approached Casey after her dish was complete. She asked her what she thought of the food. She told the instructor that the dish made her happy. She was surprised that the dish seemed mild but then had a kick at the end. And that the dish was so harmonious, and the different flavors married well.

The instructor said, "Yes, that's it, sometimes the most unlikely flavors can come together to create a beautiful outcome." Her comment kind of caught Casey by surprise because she had been thinking along the same lines.

The remainder of the trip was wonderful. Casey was starting to welcome the idea that there was possibly more to what she could see with her natural eyes. A meaning to every experience and a message in different interactions with people. She started to dig deeper and began to realize that she was finally beginning to live life. That included feeling empathetic for people and for situations. She was learning to express herself in a way she never thought possible. Was it all as a result of her conversations with Esperanza? Esperanza surely challenged her in a way that no one had before. The dynamic of the relationship was quickly shifting, and she thought that the kind of relationship they had is what people must have meant, when they said that sometimes the student becomes the teacher. She was certainly learning a lot about life and about herself.

Casey had a few days left in Thailand and as she relaxed by the pool at the resort, she was approached by a young man who worked at the hotel. The young man asked her if she would be interested in visiting an elephant sanctuary. Casey hadn't previously thought about going on an elephant excursion. The man began to explain what happens at the elephant sanctuary, but she couldn't understand much due to his thick accent and broken English. She agreed to give it a try, although it meant that she would have to extend her trip by a few days. Casey set up what she thought would be a pleasant excursion, for the following morning. The young man told her that a private shuttle would arrive at six o'clock, to take her on the two-hour ride to the sanctuary. The van arrived promptly, the following morning just as the young man had promised.

As Casey loaded her bags onto the van, she was greeted by a few other Americans who had just arrived in Thailand; they were all very nice. A young couple that she met were a little friendlier than the others and started up a conversation with her immediately. They began to ask her questions like, if it was her first time visiting a sanctuary. She replied, "Yes, this is my first visit." Casey still didn't know what she had signed up for. She envisioned the sanctuary to be a zoo like setting. As she continued her conversation with the young couple, she quickly realized that her visual was far from what she was about to experience.

"This is our third time visiting the sanctuary," the young lady said.

Her husband then interjected, "We came for the first-time last year and have been back a few times since, we love it!"

The enthusiasm coming from the young couple made Casey curious. The van was filled with people who came solely for the purpose of going to the sanctuary. They were not there to be a standard tourist, as Casey was. She felt a bit misinformed, but her curiosity grew stronger as the young couple shared their previous experiences. The ride to the sanctuary was pretty rough; and it was literally in the middle of nowhere. She had no idea where they were going. At moments during the ride she felt a little anxious and not in a good way. They finally arrived there; when a young man, the groundskeeper, greeted the group as they exited the van. He showed them around the grounds and took them to a tent, where they would be staying. The accommodations were very modest. They essentially would be sleeping on the ground, in the extreme heat. Casey was not prepared for such modest accommodations, it was a hard pill to swallow, especially because she had just come from a five-star resort. But there wasn't much she could do about it then, she would be there for the next few days.

The group was greeted with a traditional Thai breakfast called joke, a thick porridge, made by the groundskeeper and other volunteers. They were given a brief itinerary for the day.

"Work will start promptly at nine o'clock," the groundskeeper said.

"Work?" Casey asked him. "I did not sign up to work," she mumbled to herself.

She took a few bites of the joke and then she settled in as much as she could. She sat inside the tent for a few more minutes and then she saw the others heading out to a river bank. She grabbed her water bottle and followed the others out, into the unknown. As she started on her journey, she could see other groups of people working with elephants. There was a station set up where a team was administering medical care. There was a feeding station where she could see people feeding the elephants grass and fruit. Casey's group was assigned to the river. As they arrived, there were a row of elephants lined up. She didn't know what they were supposed to do with the elephants.

A woman with muddy boots, came out of the river to explain the morning activity. She explained that they would be giving the elephants a bath in the river. Casey was not prepared for the activity but was willing to try it. She put a pair of boots on and entered the water, she was a little frightened by the elephants. She had only seen elephants at the zoo and never face to face at such close proximity with one. That morning she would literally be face to face with one. The one they called, *Survivor*, was rescued just a year earlier. The elephant was a female, an older elephant. She was used as an entertainment elephant for American tourists. Once she heard the story of how Survivor was mistreated, and eventually rescued, Casey began to understand why people were so passionate about caring for them at the sanctuary.

Survivor was Casey's assigned elephant at the river. She was instructed to bathe her and so she did. Survivor looked at her with her sad eyes and somehow Casey could feel all that the elephant had endured. She was suddenly reminded of Esperanza. Maybe that was the emotion that she was missing. That missing piece to her songs and perhaps her own life. At that moment she decided that she would give Survivor her full attention and proceeded to touch the elephant in such a way, that the elephant could feel the love and compassion that she felt towards her.

As the days went on, Casey spent time feeding and assisting the medics with caring for the other elephants. The entire experience affected her in a way she didn't expect, and she returned home a little different. As she returned back from winter break, she couldn't wait to share her experience with Esperanza. When Esperanza wasn't present in class on the first day back from break, Ms. Lawson called her house to check in on her, as it was rare that she missed school. Esperanza's mom, Lisa explained that her daughter wasn't in school because their grandmother, Esperanza's great grandmother, was very ill; the family was spending as much time with her as possible. Nana Ofelia was a ninety-nine-year-old woman. She was the center of the family, the matriarch who was loved by all. "I am so sorry to hear that Lisa," Ms. Lawson sincerely said. "Please let me know if I can do anything to help." Lisa told her that Esperanza would probably appreciate a visit from her later in the week. And so, she agreed to come by on Friday.

Esperanza entered Nana's bedroom early Thursday morning. As she entered the room, she heard the voice of a man that she didn't recognize. The man stood up, she could tell that he was tall.

"Hello, I'm Leo." Leo was Esperanza's dad's cousin.

"I have heard so much about you," she said.

"I hope it was good, young lady."

"My dad says that you are the toughest cop in New York City." Leo proudly smiled at her description of himself.

"Well young lady, I am a tough, but fair cop."

Esperanza accepted his description as she sat down at Nana's bedside.

"I will leave you two alone," Leo told her.

"Thank you, I will only be a few minutes, I know that there are a lot of people outside who want to see her."

Nana overheard the conversation between the two of them and was pleased that they had finally met. "Nana can you hear me?" Esperanza softly whispered.

"Yes, mija I can hear you."

"Nana, I know you are ready to fly, and I want you to fly but not before you have one more talk with me, I need your golden words, just once more."

Nana Ofelia was someone that Esperanza looked up to and she loved her with all her heart. Nana loved her just the same, they shared a special bond. From the time Esperanza could remember, Nana shared stories about her life and about how it was to live in the old days. Whenever Esperanza felt discouraged because she was blind, she would share her frustration with her. She wouldn't share her frustrations with her parents because she didn't want to make them feel bad. Nana would tell her that her inability to see was actually a gift. She explained that it was a gift because she could smell, feel, and hear better than anyone else. So, she may have lacked one gift but in turn she gained three. Nana always made her feel better and inspired her to be great. She reassured her that her disability was not a reason to be less than she was meant to be. Nana explained that because she had the gift of sight, she could see greatness in Esperanza.

"Mija, we are not to waste the gifts and talents we have been given." "And you my dear have many great gifts and talents, remember, there is *no one* like you." As Nana sat upright, in her favorite pink pajama top, Esperanza held her hand tight. Esperanza could smell the fragrance of the flowers at her bedside. The fragrances were strong and smelled like an entire garden to her. She asked Nana to tell her about the time she saw the beautiful rainbow over the ocean in Hawaii. Nana used every descriptive word in her vocabulary to share not what the sight looked like, but rather what it felt like. It was stories like that, that somehow eased Esperanza in a way that nothing else could. Esperanza gained a broad insight into explaining how things felt or were supposed to feel. Over exaggerated at times, she learned it all from Nana. She had a way of imparting wisdom into all of her grandchildren, from the oldest to the youngest. She recognized just how different they all were. She wanted to make sure that they would have those special moments, in which they would realize that her narrative was for the greater good; each word filled with great purpose.

"Mija, always remember that I will be your eyes when you feel like you need that extra gift to be complete." "I will be there to guide you through life by every word I have spoken to you."

"I know you will be my eyes Nana."

As the week went on Nana Ofelia grew weaker. She had several visitors and all her grandchildren came to say their good byes. She spent the week depositing words of wisdom into the lives of others. Some conversations short and sweet and others a bit more intense. And by Friday, she took her final breath surrounded by her loved ones. Esperanza was completely heart broken, she had never felt such sorrow in her young life. She felt that someone had taken a knife to her heart.

Friday evening Ms. Lawson came to visit the family. Esperanza held Ms. Lawson extremely tight that evening. And Ms. Lawson felt the sorrow that the thirteen-year-old felt. They spent some time together and after a few hours, Ms. Lawson was able to get Esperanza to feel a sense of comfort. At that moment, Ms. Lawson knew just how special Nana Ofelia was to the young lady and the unique relationship they shared. She later told Esperanza that she wished she had the opportunity to meet her great grandmother before she passed. She believed that the woman must have been someone truly special. How could a woman with such profound words not be? Ms. Lawson could tell that Nana certainly had a lasting impact on Esperanza. And by Esperanza sharing some words of wisdom and stories with her, it now impacted her own life.

As the year went on, the friendship between the two continued to blossom. Ms. Lawson provided Esperanza with a sense of feeling valued, even though she was just a kid. They shared mutual respect and admiration for one another. Ms. Lawson finally shared her experience with Esperanza about the Thailand trip. She was amazed and thrilled that Ms. Lawson was beginning to feel things, instead of just seeing them, or hearing them, or by touching them. Esperanza continued to share some of her wisdom that she gained from Nana, with Ms. Lawson. Ms. Lawson found the lessons and stories to be inspirational. She learned a great deal from the young lady. She reflected on things in her own life that needed construction as she continued her journey to her, Lifelong List, with the encouragement of the young lady of course. Who would have thought that the ripple effects of wisdom and life experience, could impact a total stranger? She certainly had a lot of life to look forward to.

Esperanza looked like an angel, the angels that her mother said sang in heaven, the ones she was kissed by. And as she walked across the stage to perform at the school talent show, Ms. Lawson looked on as a proud friend would. The poise and confidence Esperanza exuded, would make anyone proud just to know her. And as she sat down at the piano, she said, "I want to dedicate this original piece to those who love, those who inspire, and to those who are willing to be the eyes for those who can't see." "We all have gifts and talents that we must not waist; this song is called, *Seasons of Hope*."

That day Casey heard the most emotional song she had ever heard. And in that special moment, she could feel what seasons of hope felt like. It felt like a young wise girl, it felt like a grandmother's gentle touch, it felt like a look from an abused animal, it felt like a lonely soul, it felt like a rainbow in the sky. And with all these emotions, it caused her to smile because she finally experienced feeling, something real. And she learned it from a child. And somehow, she accepted the fact that it was okay to feel the good or bad and the sometimes in between. It was okay to feel every emotion, as long as she felt something. Casey Lawson had a new-found zeal for life. She was now able to live a life filled with wonder and adventure, the very things that were missing, thanks to Esperanza, and the profound words of a woman she had never met.

CHAPTER THREE

....

Love Defined

IT WAS A COLD, FRIDAY NIGHT, IN MID-DECEMBER. FIONA WAS WATCH-
ING HER FAVORITE MOVIE, THE HOLIDAY. She especially loved the
scene when the old Hollywood producer's character, explained to
Kate Winslet's character, what a *Meet-Cute* was. As Fiona understood
it, the Meet-Cute, was a moment in a movie that a romantic connection occurs. It's a moment where two people meet in a strange
or quirky way. It was a single moment; a moment Fiona wondered
would ever happen to her.

Fiona thought about what her Meet-Cute, might be like. Maybe she would have locked her keys in her car, when out of nowhere,
a broad-shouldered man would appear. He would have flawlessly
slicked back hair and would be wearing a white muscle shirt, where
she could see every last curvature of his toned muscles. He would be
there to assist her in her time of need. She would gaze into his light
brown eyes, as he pulled a hanger from out of the trunk of his fiery
red mustang. He would unwind the hanger to make it linear, as he
looked at her with a starry gaze. The gaze would be monumental,
and she would immediately know that he was her Knight in Shining

Armor. And boom, there you have it, the Meet-Cute. After the meet, the two of them would fall deep into summer love. They would spend their nights, enjoying lovely dinners that the light brown eyed man had prepared.

But that only happens in movies, Fiona thought, as her vision slowly faded away. She was infatuated with falling in love but doubted that genuine, long lasting love would ever knock on her door. That is, if love was real at all. At least up until that point she hadn't seen or experienced something that she would consider real love.

Fiona was a very accomplished twenty-nine-year-old. She was highly educated, deeply cultured and well spoken. She had never been in love with anyone, except maybe her first crush, but that was just a teenaged sort of love. She had a lot of short-term affairs with different men. She loved the thrill and excitement of being with a new man. And even though she was free to date around, inwardly she desired a more authentic experience, a real Meet-Cute with someone she could have for eternity. She imagined that her grandparents, Nana Ofelia and Grandpa Leo, had experienced a Meet-Cute. They found real love. But that was back in the day, she thought.

She thought that things were different then because most woman needed men, to be the provider. In contrast, modern day women take care of themselves, therefore they really don't need a man. She thought that in some ways this new aged thinking was unfortunate but nonetheless, she was a modern woman. She wasn't necessarily seeking love out, but felt that if it magically appeared, she would be open to the possibility. "I would like to consider myself a *hopeful romantic,*" she told her friends. Fiona was an exquisite woman, she had a unique look about her and people often guessed wrong at her ethnicity. She was a Mexican-American, with roots from the Southwest. She was fair skinned, a red head, with bountiful freckles and green eyes. Fiona was a successful woman, working at a prestigious law firm in Chicago's city center. She was always well dressed, with a standard daily look of business suits, black pumps, and her hair pulled back into a tight low bun. She occasionally wore the pearls that Nana Ofelia gave to her, when she left Colorado.

Fiona had been recruited by the firm because she had built quite a reputation back in Denver, and just as she expected, her career quickly catapulted when she moved to Chicago. She knew that she would eventually make partner at the firm. She was a tough attorney who rarely lost a case. Being offered an opportunity to work for such a successful firm was a hard opportunity to pass up. She was young and free and enjoyed making new friends and feeling the heartbeat of different cities. She quickly adjusted and relished living in Chicago. She rapidly made friends and was often the center of attention at any gathering. Not only was she outwardly beautiful but she had a charismatic personality, which made it nearly impossible not to want to be around her.

Fiona wasn't an over achiever growing up, in fact she was just an average student. But she was determined to be someone of significance. She was quiet and observant as a child, and so she was most certainly making up for her timid nature, in her adult years. She had finally gained the confidence to speak and assumed her blossoming character with a Princess Diana, sort of grace. She was the only Latina, in an otherwise diverse firm. Fiona often worked late nights during the week; she felt uncomfortable with starting tasks that she couldn't finish. At times it felt as though she lived at the office. She thought perhaps she should buy a futon and just sleep there. On occasion, she would doze off with her head on her desk, Cartier pen still in hand. She was often over critical of herself and a bit of a perfectionist. No one really knew that about her though; she seemed relaxed and put together to others.

Prior to the move to Chicago, she had an affair with an older, married man named Keith. He was a fellow attorney that Fiona was completely infatuated with. Deep down she knew the relationship was detrimental to her, another reason the job offer in Chicago was timely. She wanted desperately to get away from Keith, even though she cared for him. He was a master manipulator with his words and seductive ways. She found herself in a conundrum, a tangled web of deceit, concealed by charming words and puppy dog eyes. She didn't know how to untangle herself from the web and didn't understand why she allowed the affair to last so long. She was certain that he would never leave his wife for her, nor did she necessarily want him to. The affair wasn't intentional, as Fiona was unaware that Keith was a married man, but he had already spun his web. She knew that he was not a good man, but he somehow gave her the high that comes with being in love, even if it was superficial.

After the move, she was relieved that she had finally escaped from his web and she reflected on how quickly those things happen. Was she a bad person for allowing the affair to continue after she learned of the marriage? Had she not had enough self-control to resist his scent and his touch? Fiona knew that it was wrong to get involved with a married man, she felt disappointed in herself and learned a great deal from the affair. She vowed never to allow herself to entertain the thought of being with someone who belonged to someone else, ever again. She had also learned a lot about men from Keith and from other men who crossed her path. Some days she hated men, other days she longed for companionship. Deep down she wanted a family of her own but wasn't sure it would ever happen. She often doubted that she would even have children. Most of her friends from high school and college were already mothers. She wasn't like some modern-day women who purposely bore a child, as a single parent. She thought that those women were somewhat selfish, and she valued a traditional family unit.

Wintertime in Chicago can be harsh; the winds coming off Lake Michigan are unforgiving. Fiona dreaded the walk from the office back to her apartment building. The weather is the only thing she disliked about the city. One night during the holiday season, Fiona was finally leaving the office at close to ten o'clock pm. The cleaning crew was beginning to clean the twenty-fifth floor of the office building. She had noticed an older lady a few other times but never spoke to her. The cleaning lady must have been in her late sixties, Fiona guessed. She could see that the woman was tired but took such pride in her job, not overlooking one streak on the mirrors or windows. That winter evening, Fiona was glaring out the window at the falling snowflakes. It looked very beautiful and she admired it for a moment, until she remembered that the five-block walk back to her apartment would be a challenge.

"May I clean this office now?" the lady asked.

Fiona answered, "Sure, I will be leaving shortly, but you can start now."

The woman acknowledged her by nodding her head. Her accent was strong, and her hands showed the many years of hard work she had done, for people who probably didn't care enough to know her name. She was a face, a face of an uneducated, lower class, immigrant woman. Irrespective of how she was profiled, there was a story behind her face. The fact was that the woman was a warrior, a dedicated wife and someone's mother. Because she was a cleaning lady, she accepted that a face is probably all she would ever be considered, to the people she served.

No one, not one single person, had ever held a conversation with her in the past five years that she had been working at the twenty-five-story building. She became accustomed to holding her head down when coming into contact with the high-class attorneys who worked there. She found most of them to be rude, the ones who weren't rude simply never went out of their way to acknowledge her. She expected that Fiona would be another rude attorney, and so she went on about her duties that night. Fiona could see the woman was struggling with a large tin trash can and so she went over to lift it up for her. The woman was taken aback and quickly held Fiona's arm, in an attempt to stop her.

"My boss not allow this," she told Fiona, in broken English.

Fiona looked puzzled, as if to say, she didn't care about the woman's boss. She picked up the trash can and held it in place until every last piece of crumbled up paper and every last apple core was gone. The woman didn't speak and didn't need to because Fiona could see the relief and gratitude she wore on her face.

"What is your name?" Fiona asked the woman.

"Isabella," she replied.

"Pleasure to meet you Isabella." The woman nodded her head, to reciprocate the sentiment, and then Fiona ventured out to meet the falling snowflakes.

Fiona saw Isabella around the same time for the next few nights. Fiona was working on a very important case, which required additional hours of research. At times she became unfocused; she would stare out the window and think about how different her life would be if she was married. She thought about how she would work less because she would want to spend the winter nights with her love. She thought about how their love would let nothing come between them and every time they saw each other would be like the first time their eyes met; she imagined so much. On occasion, Isabella would unintendedly see Fiona wandering off to what seemed like another world; she wondered what had Fiona in such deep thoughts.

As Isabella picked up the heavy trash can, she felt a strong hand help her lift it up. This time she didn't say anything to Fiona, just a subtle smile and a hand over hand gesture of gratitude. Over the next several weeks, Isabella noticed that the large heavy trash can was emptied before she got a chance to throw it. The two women would occasionally see each other, and Fiona would consistently make it a point to acknowledge Isabella. Isabella would leave Fiona homemade alfajores, Peruvian cookies, native to Isabella's home land, on her desk. The two had a mutual respect for one another. They finally began to talk from time to time and the conversations became a little more frequent and extended as time went on. Fiona learned more about Isabella and her family. She was curious as to why Isabella was still working at her age and asked her about it one night.

"My husband is unable to work, and we need the money to live on." She shared that her husband had cancer and that the medical bills had been overwhelming. Fiona felt empathy for the Isabella and soon she started leaving an envelope with money for her at her desk; she disguised the money in a birthday card. She knew Isabella would not accept her gift and she also didn't want her to get in trouble, therefore she thought it best to disguise it.

"Why are you giving me money?" "It is not my birthday," Isabella said after opening the envelope.

Fiona replied, "We should celebrate life every day, so today *is* your birthday."

Isabella felt ashamed, and for a moment regretted telling Fiona about her situation. But her heart was grateful as she could really use the money, so she accepted the gift. Once a week Fiona left a birthday card at her desk for her.

"You remind me of someone," Fiona told Isabella one night. "My Nana Ofelia was a housekeeper." "She would tell me about how hard she worked cleaning rich people's houses; most of the people didn't treat her very well."

Isabella didn't completely understand Fiona, but she knew that Fiona was a very good lady, unlike some of the other people who worked in the office. "My nana had hands like yours, tired hands." As Fiona described Nana's hands, Isabella looked at her own and realized that her hands were indeed tired. "My nana taught me that I should treat everyone with respect." Nana had told Fiona stories about how poorly she was treated; she taught her to never look down on someone based on their profession. Fiona promised her that she never would. In fulfillment of her promise to her, she went out of her way to look service workers in the eye and thank them. She was genuine about how she felt about them.

"Your grandmother sounds like she was a beautiful lady." "I

taught my son the same things," Isabella said.

As Fiona left the office that night, she smiled as she saw the tissue folded like a fan on her desk. After years working as a housekeeper, Nana would still fold up tissues like fans in the boxes around her house. Fiona assumed it was out of habit after so many years, she smiled at the little reminders and memories she had of her. It made her happy to know that because of those little reminders, Nana would always be with her.

One night she overheard a colleague yelling at Isabella, accusing her of stealing his wallet. Fiona heard the commotion and went over to inquire. As her colleague yelled at Isabella, he was close enough that she was sure Isabella could smell his breath, Fiona began looking for the wallet, which she found behind the man's desk.

"Is this your wallet?" Fiona furiously asked.

Her colleague grabbed his wallet and said, "Thank you Fiona, you know how these cleaning people can be."

"I don't know what you mean," Fiona replied. "This woman has been nothing but kind to me."

Her colleague was surprised by her position. Fiona said, "You really need to learn how to treat people like human beings!" Nana taught her that being a decent person was the bare minimum, she needed to be better than just a decent human being.

"Always, always treat people well, even if they don't treat you the same, and do your best to help those in need," these words spoken by Nana, had been embedded into Fiona's mind and heart, throughout her life.

Later on, that night Isabella thanked her for intervening and hugged Fiona tight and said, "You are a very humble and more than a decent human being." Fiona went to sleep feeling like she made Nana proud of the person she had become.

There was a vicious storm a few days before Christmas and the news reported a delay of flights. Instead of attempting to catch a flight back to Colorado, Fiona decided it would probably be best to stay in Chicago for the holiday. On Christmas Eve, Fiona figured she might as well work instead of staying home feeling sad about not being able to see her family. Besides, she had plenty of research to do for the Cook case that she was assigned to. Isabella was also working that night. Isabella brought Fiona a gift, wrapped ever so beautifully in gold paper.

"Open it now Fiona."

Fiona agreed to open the gift because she could see the anticipation on Isabella's face. She was immediately grateful for the gesture, coming from someone who had so little. After carefully ripping through the gold wrapping, she pulled out a bracelet from inside a box. "Thank you, it's one of the most unique pieces of jewelry I have ever seen."

Isabella explained to her what the bracelet signified, "The beads on this bracelet are Huayruro beads. Huayruro beads will bring positive energy, love, happiness and good fortune to you, my friend. These beads grow from a plant in Peru and the beads have been worn by Incan royalty for hundreds of years all through South America. You deserve to wear these beads like the Queens have. You my friend, are a Queen."

Fiona was grateful for such a thoughtful gift and she gave her a heartfelt hug. "Where are you spending Christmas?" Isabella asked Fiona. Fiona explained that she would not be able to get back home to her family in time due to flight delays. "Please have dinner in my home with me and my husband." Fiona didn't know if she was asking her or telling her and felt as though she should not decline the kind invitation.

The two of them caught a cab to a tiny house on Chicago's south side, one of the worst neighborhoods in the city. Upon arriving, the two of them had to shovel a pathway into the courtyard area, to gain access to the house.

"Do you do this every night?" Fiona asked.

"Yes, I do."

After about a half an hour of shoveling, the ladies entered the tiny house; the aroma of something wonderful filled it. Fiona could tell that it was the kind of food that had been simmering all day. *Amorcito*, Isabella called out to her husband. There on a blue recliner, sat a very sweet old man. Isabella walked over and gave her husband a hug and kiss on the cheek. Fiona could immediately see the love they had for one another. They looked into each other's eyes and smiled, as if to say, *we made it another day.* Her husband, Rogelio, kissed her on her forehead, something he had done since they were young; Fiona found it endearing.

"Come," Isabella told Fiona as she motioned her over to meet Rogelio. "This is my husband."

"It is a pleasure to finally meet you, young lady," he said.

Fiona attempted a formal hand shake, but instead he gently grabbed her hand, and pulled it close to his chest, as if he had previously met her. Fiona felt foolish for trying to be so formal, he seemed like a sweet man; he had the softest eyes. She could see that he was not well, but he was gentle and kind, in a way that would be visible to virtually anyone.

"Dinner is ready, let's sit." Isabella then grabbed the wheelchair that was next to the recliner. She picked her husband up to help him onto the chair, as Fiona looked on, unsure what she should do. As they entered the small dining room area, Isabella ensured that Fiona and her husband were settled in. She then went to the kitchen and brought the food out to the table.

"May I help?" Fiona asked.

Isabella shook her head and said, "No, no, no, you are a guest."

Fiona felt bad for not helping but she knew that she could not convince her otherwise. She could see that Isabella had a servant's heart, and that she was just happy to have a guest in her home. Isabella displayed such pride in everything from the detailed table décor, to the delicious food. After the food was brought out, the couple bowed their heads and then they shared a moment of silence.

Fiona thought they were going to say a prayer, but with no words spoken, they prayed in silence, in their own way. She thought it to be different but sat in reverence at their actions.

Fiona realized that it was the first time she had a sit-down dinner with an actual family, since moving to Chicago. She attended many formal business dinners with clients and sat at various bars with friends while sharing a deep-dish pizza. But there was nothing like a home cooked meal. She felt comfortable with the couple, it felt familiar and she realized how much she missed her own family. She was saddened for a moment but felt a connection to Isabella and Rogelio, and so she was going to take advantage of the time. The table was filled with conversation as they enjoyed their meal together. Isabella must have told Rogelio everything she knew about Fiona. Over the course of dinner, he would occasionally caress his wife's hand; they were the sweetest couple. Fiona wondered if she would be blessed to have a love like theirs, in her lifetime. The couple shared the story about how they met and married. They had known each other all their lives. They grew up in the same village and were close friends. Back in Peru, they married very young, at fifteen and seventeen years old; they had never been apart.

"I wouldn't know what to do without my *Amorcito*," Isabella said.

They had arrived in the United States about five years earlier. They had come because they knew Rogelio could get better health care to treat his cancer, in the United States. The region they were from was still yet pretty underdeveloped and the healthcare wasn't advanced enough to provide him with the services he needed. It was a good thing they came to the United States, as he was now cancer free. But the treatments had worn on his old fragile body. Isabella was working and doing her best to keep them going; the medical bills they incurred were astronomical. They knew that they would never pay the bills off entirely, but they were honest, hardworking people, and they would do their best to satisfy their debt. They were just grateful that Rogelio was cancer free.

Isabella talked about their son, Rogelio Jr. He was finishing his studies in Peru, and soon was going to be a doctor. They explained that they had to hold on a little longer; their son would be coming to take care of them. Fiona was impressed by the fact that they had raised such a bright and ambitious son. She herself knew the hard work and determination it took to pursue such a prestigious profession. The three of them enjoyed their time, sharing stories of love and about life. Fiona felt such admiration for the lovely couple. Isabella recollected how well Rogelio had always taken care of her. She shared about times when they had little or no food in their village in Peru. "When Rogelio had his last piece of bread, he would give it to me; we had many struggles, but we kept our promise to each other." Isabella appreciated the man, who now sat in a wheelchair, unable to do the things he once did.

"I am honored to take care of such a wonderful man. That is what true love is. I have nothing, if I don't have this man. Every experience I have ever had, would mean nothing, if he wasn't by my side."

Fiona had never seen such a genuine love. She wished she could have witnessed her grandparents sharing the kind of love that the couple shared.

As the night ended, Fiona felt such a warmth, deep in her soul, she sincerely thanked them for making it one of the most memorable holidays she had in Chicago. "You have been very kind to me, you have a special heart," Isabella said. Fiona hugged the two of them as she headed to her apartment. The next morning, as Fiona got out of her bed filled with expensive down pillows, she thought about how challenging it must be for Isabella to take care of her husband. She knew that Rogelio needed around the clock care and what a challenge that must have been for them, especially while Isabella was working. She decided that she should help them in any way she could. She got dressed and headed to the store to buy them some groceries.

"Tonight, I will cook for the two of you," she said as she arrived at their house. Fiona made them a delicious meal and the couple was pleasantly surprised that she would go out of her way not only to feed them, but more importantly to visit with them; after all, they too had no family in Chicago. Fiona continued going over to visit and bring them weekly groceries. Dinner would occur a couple of times a week. "It must have been difficult watching your husband fighting cancer," Fiona said.

"Yes, it has been very difficult but taking care of someone you love is a privilege, my husband used to be a strong man. He was a charming and handsome man, and he still is. And like any other couple, we have had some difficult times. Only the strongest love could help us overcome some of the lowest times in our lives. We have not always been blessed with money, but we have been blessed with family and good health through the years."

Fiona learned a great deal from Isabella and it wasn't a bad thing to learn some of her amazing Peruvian recipes simultaneously. She also learned a lot more about what love really looked like, by their example. She had never witnessed such a strong bond in a marriage from anyone and aspired to have the same one day. She thought that this kind of love must have been what Nana was talking about when she told her of the greatest love she had ever known, her grandfather Leo. Eventually, Fiona shared her hopes with the couple about finding a love of her own. After learning of her desires, they encouraged her to be patient. "A love of your own will find you in its own time." "We have a great love story and you too will have your great love story." These were the words they would tell her repeatedly, and Fiona held on tightly to their words. She concluded that they must had known something about love since they had lived their entire lives making each other happy.

Springtime was approaching, and Rogelio mentioned that before he began cancer treatment, he usually spent most of his days in the garden of the courtyard. Fiona promised she would help him plant because he wasn't physically able to tend to the garden like he used to.

"I am very saddened by the way these flowers look," Rogelio said. The winter was harsh and some of the perennials weren't even growing; she could see the frustration on his face.

"We can do this together," she assured him.

The man looked at her with sincere eyes as if to ask, *where did you come from?* He thought she was heaven sent. The next few weeks, Fiona spent many evenings at their house, planting and learning a lot about flowers. She had never gardened before and was determined not to let the kind man down. The two of them became very close and she grew to love him like a father.

"Sometimes in life, storms will come and destroy your garden, but you can plant again; sometimes the universe wipes away the old to allow something new to blossom, but you must continue to water your garden every day."

Fiona agreed with Rogelio and listened closely to his daily parables. In some strange way she was learning to fall in love with life just by being around he and Isabella. Fiona appreciated the wise lessons that the couple had taught her. It reminded her how much she missed Nana Ofelia. Rogelio asked, "Why is it that you are so good to my wife?" "She is a cleaner and you are a *fancy* lawyer."

Fiona explained that Nana was a cleaning lady. "Isabella's hands look like my nana's hands and that's what drew me to her."

She told him about how Nana taught her to respect everyone, no matter what they did for a living. Fiona knew how hard Nana worked and she saw the same ethic in Isabella. Not only did Fiona respect these women but she also looked up to them. "Isabella and my nana are some of hardest working women I have ever known." "I work with my mind, and to me that is much easier than how hard they have worked with their bare hands; I can only hope to be as well respected one day." Rogelio was pleased by what Fiona said, he thought the world of her. They were a blessing to one another but moreover Fiona somehow believed that the couple was sent to her by Nana for a reason.

Soon springtime was in full bloom and so was Rogelio's garden. The smile that the flowers put on his face was priceless. Fiona felt so much pride in the many hours of work she had done to help the man regain joy. She wanted to do something nice for the couple as their anniversary was in May; a special one at that. They would be celebrating fifty years of marriage.

"This surely calls for a celebration!"

Fiona told them that she wanted to plan a special dinner to celebrate. They were elated that she wanted to celebrate them. Isabella loved Fiona as if she was her own daughter and their relationship held such a lovely fragrance. Fiona prepared for their special night for weeks, she wanted the evening to be magical. It was a warm Saturday in May, and Isabella and Rogelio were getting dressed for the evening. Isabella finally let her long, perfectly silver hair down. Rogelio wore a vibrant handwoven dress shirt directly from Peru. Fiona arranged for the two of them to meet in the courtyard at seven o'clock.

She had transformed the courtyard, and it looked like a scene straight out of a movie. It was decorated with hanging lights and she even found a way to light up the garden, so that every flower colorfully radiated. She made a small wedding cake from scratch, and not just any cake. Fiona called her sister Clarissa back home to ask her for Nana's cake recipe. Since it was Nana's special recipe, Fiona knew the cake would be magical. She surely went the extra mile to bring her vision for the celebration to life.

The garden was filled with butterflies that evening, not just small butterflies but full-grown monarchs. They were majestically flying around like they had been invited to the celebration; the setting was absolutely whimsical. Fiona had the couples wedding picture restored and blown up to fit in a nice custom vintage looking frame. She placed the photo next to the cake and as she was putting the final touches on, she stepped back to look at the photo. It was perfection; the picture alone told a story of everlasting love and perseverance. She felt extremely blessed to be a part of their lives. As Fiona lit up the candles around the cake, a ladybug suddenly landed on her ring finger; she was flattered by the landing. She then realized that the beads on the bracelet she was wearing, the one that Isabella had given her, resembled ladybugs. Fiona shook her head in amazement at the moment she was in. And as the ladybug stood still on her finger, she thought about all she had learned over the past few months.

Fiona's heart was full and although at times she felt lonely, that day she was filled with love by seeing the smiles of the lovely couple. They had taught her more about love than she could have imagined. She knew that one day she would experience that same kind of love. And as she made a wish before the ladybug flew away, she asked the universe for a moment of genuine love with someone who would kiss her on her forehead, the way Rogelio kissed Isabella. And just as the ladybug spread its wings to fly, a man walked towards her.

"Hello, I am Rogelio," the man said. "You are just as they described you."

She then realized that the man was Rogelio and Isabella's son. She had asked Isabella to invite him to the celebration, but she said he would not be able to make it. Fiona was speechless at the sight of the handsome man. He was tall, slender, wore glasses, and nothing like she envisioned him to be. Fiona felt like she experienced her Meet-Cute as the ladybug flew away. The two of them locked eyes and hugged each other like they had been long lost friends; it felt foreign yet natural at the same time.

"Fiona may I come out?" Isabella asked. Fiona was so distracted that she had to take a deep breath and regain her composure.

"Can you bring your father out of the house through the back door?" she asked Rogelio Jr.

"I will signal your mother to come out when I see your father near the garden."

The groom looked as happy as Fiona imagined he looked on his wedding day. And Isabella looked so amazingly regal, a woman of strength and dignity. The bride and groom stared at each other from opposite ends of the courtyard. The garden was transformed to a magical place where the two of them could share a profound moment that they would remember for the rest of their lives. Music played in the background, and Isabella walked over to her groom; she was shining brighter than the lights that illuminated the flowers. As she drew closer, her groom gave her a single rose as he stood out of his wheelchair. Isabella gasped in disbelief that her husband suddenly had the strength to stand on his own. With a gentle smile Isabella said, *Amorcito.* The two shared a sincere embrace and a dance that they never wanted to end. They danced as if they were the only ones on the entire planet.

And on that magical night, as the butterflies soared high, Fiona finally witnessed images of real love and she believed at that moment that anything was possible. Perhaps true love really did exist, perhaps love was standing in the courtyard with her...perhaps her moment had finally come.

CHAPTER FOUR

Julian Rises

"YOU ARE JUST MISUNDERSTOOD MIJO," NANA OFELIA OFTEN TOLD JULIAN, WHEN SHE WAS ALIVE. Julian could never quite understand if that was a positive or negative sentiment. Nana explained that she too was often times misunderstood, even by her own family. But nonetheless, her words stuck with him and he would often be comforted by the sentiment when he found himself in certain situations. He thought to himself, *this is what Nana must've meant when she said I am misunderstood.*

Julian was a very unique twenty-one-year old. Tall and awkwardly slim, he stood well over six feet tall. He was a poet, a painter, an artist. Nana Ofelia raised him in the tiny house on Sherman Street where she had raised all four of her children. And although the grandchildren visited Nana often, Julian was the only grandchild she had a hand in raising. When Nana Ofelia passed away she left the house to Julian. He had no idea that he would inherit the house, until months after she passed away. Initially, he didn't want the house because he knew other family members would resent him for it, especially Uncle Hector.

Uncle Hector was the oldest son, who forever felt entitled. Julian didn't like confrontation and wondered why she chose him, if she knew he would face opposition. She could've chosen anyone, he thought. And Julian agreed that even though Uncle Hector was a full grown spoiled, entitled brat, that maybe it was right that he should have taken possession of the house.

Nana Ofelia raised Julian because his mother, Marisol, couldn't handle him as a young boy. He was full of energy, so much in fact that it often led him into trouble. He seemed to do better with Nana, perhaps because she had more patience. And so, she raised him since he was six years old. Nana Ofelia worked with Julian a lot, she spent many hours talking to him and giving him the attention that he needed. His behavior seemed to become much calmer as he grew. Julian loved Nana more than life itself; he took her passing very hard. His entire life, dreams and aspirations became a blur when she left, even though he was at peace with how he took care of her. He spent day and night tending to her needs. He only felt some relief when his Aunt Martha came during the mornings. The last week before she passed, Aunt Martha and her daughter Fiona, from Chicago, stayed at the house. Julian was glad to have them there, as he needed the support. Julian knew that Nana was happy to have him close to her the remaining days of her life, in fact he held her hand until her very last breath.

Growing up, Julian was introverted, he mainly focused on developing his artistry. He wasn't very interested in having friends, except for Daisy, a neighbor, who also lived with her grandmother, Mrs. Chavez. Julian was a spectacular poet and artist; he in fact was offered three full ride scholarships to different art schools. He wrote poetry almost daily and had several notebooks filled with poems and inspirational art. He was definitely misunderstood by people, at times even by his own family. He was grateful for Daisy's friendship because he felt like she was one of the only people, besides Nana, who fully understood him. Or at least the both of them acted as though they did.

Julian and Daisy were very close, and they spent a lot of time together. Daily bike rides around the neighborhood was one of their favorite things to do, and they had done so since they learned to pedal a bike. They knew the neighborhood like the back of their hands, every alley and every hidden corner. They spent many evenings sitting on the railroad tracks, hoping that a train wouldn't travel through. As they sat on the old rusty tracks, they talked about everything from art, to traveling, to politics. Daisy found Julian to be the most intelligent person that she knew. Even if his bohemian style and unruly curly hair would suggest otherwise. Julian taught her a lot about life and he appreciated the fact that someone would listen to him and his crazy ideas. Julian loved to read and sometimes they would sit in the park and he would tell her about a book he read, quoting the most insightful words. He was somewhat of a nerd but indeed a brilliant mind. Daisy thought that Julian was a genius, she truly believed that.

The year the two of them graduated, Daisy was indecisive about whether she should leave the state to go to college or stay in state. She finally decided to leave, and Julian was heartbroken but understood she had dreams and supported her decision. He never showed her just how much he didn't want her to leave. Especially because she was a huge support system after Nana passed. And now he felt completely abandoned by the two women who were such a crucial part of his life.

That summer was life changing for him. Since Nana had passed away and Daisy left within just a matter of months, he found himself alone and wondering what would be next for him. He declined his scholarships because he knew he would not be able to go with such an unclear mind and a heavy heart. He thought it unfair for any school to invest in someone who would not be able to give them their all. Some critical family members, especially Uncle Hector, told him that it was a waste of time to go to an art school anyway and that he needed to get a real job. Julian rarely listened to what other people said, he knew he was different and had grown accustomed to being misunderstood.

After inheriting the house, Julian spent the summer cleaning it up and making some improvements that Nana hadn't previously allowed. And with the taking down of every picture frame and taking Nana's clothes out for delivery to the second-hand store, he felt more alone than ever before. No one went over to the house anymore, partially because Uncle Hector was bitter and had an influence on the family. Julian began to resent Nana for leaving him the house. The house that was once the center of the family, no longer served the same purpose. He even contemplated selling it, so he could forget about all the memories the house held but didn't know where he would go. He never knew anywhere else but that house; that neighborhood.

Since he had decided not to attend college, he wasn't sure what he would do next, workwise. He didn't need much money to live on, the only things he would need money for was food and a few other minimal house bills. He had worked at different jobs in the neighborhood, since he was sixteen years old. He worked at the neighborhood market, waited tables at Mr. Romero's family restaurant and other odd and end jobs. He hadn't worked much his senior year though, since he was caring for Nana.

While Julian was taking a walk one sunny afternoon, he saw a sign that read *Dog Walkers Wanted*. He thought it sounded different and he liked different, so he applied. Soon enough he was on his way to being, a certified dog walker. He was great with dogs and over time became in high demand. He didn't realize how many people in the neighborhood owned dogs. The neighborhood had drastically changed over the past few years. A once highly Latino populated neighborhood was now filled with young professionals, multi-millionaires, hipsters and transplants from other states. Julian enjoyed some of the ways that the neighborhood was changing, especially the artistic vibe. It was becoming a trendy neighborhood with new art work being displayed on the new and old buildings, he appreciated it.

As he walked through various streets, he saw new houses going up and neighborhood fixtures disappearing slowly but surely. He wasn't quite sure how to feel about it, the more he paid attention, week after week. Julian was such a great walker that it wasn't uncommon for him to have upwards of five dogs at one time. He was accustomed to awkward stares from people; when they saw him passing through the neighborhood with five or six dogs in tow, he simply disregarded their stares. He was enjoying his newfound talent, he was becoming the *Dog Whisperer* of the neighborhood.

He and Daisy stayed in contact and she was continuously fascinated by his new ventures, even if sometimes a bit comical. She was relieved that he was doing something to make himself happy, as she knew how much he must have missed Nana. "You have always liked to do things out of the box," she said. He admired her for following her dreams and although he missed her dearly, he was happy that she was doing great, at New Mexico State University. He wished that she had never left Denver and felt sad to hear her voice; on occasion, he wouldn't answer her phone calls. He had mixed feelings, and her voice brought him more sadness than comfort.

Julian knew a lot of the old families in the neighborhood. He began to notice that more of them were moving out and some of the older neighbors were passing away. Their children were selling their houses quick, the area was becoming one of the most desirable neighborhoods to live in. One day Julian was passing by the park where he saw Mrs. Chavez, Daisy's grandmother, sitting on a bench. He went over to say hello, as Mrs. Chavez and Nana had been great friends for many years.

"How are you doing Mrs. Chavez?" he asked.

"I'm old and tired," she slowly answered. "The hill up to the park is getting more difficult every day, and with all the construction,

I have to walk an extra two blocks to get up here."

Julian felt empathetic towards her and said he would be happy to walk with her to keep her company, in an effort to make the walk more pleasurable. She thought it sweet and thanked him for the kind gesture.

"You know Julian, this neighborhood used to be a special place to live."

He didn't understand what she was trying to say but was attentive nonetheless. She went on to describe what the neighborhood used to be like.

"The new yoga studio on High Street used to be a shoe store owned by the Guajardo family, all of the women in the neighborhood bought their beautiful shoes from there. Every Friday morning women lined up awaiting the new shipment of shoes to come in. They showed them off at mass at St. Patrick's on Sunday morning, we had everything we needed right in our own backyard."

Julian listened to Mrs. Chavez for a long while, explaining to him how the neighborhood looked years before. "Everyone used to look out for one another; it was common for families to spend their Sunday afternoons together enjoying a meal in someone's backyard, while the children played." "The burgers at The Burger Hut were twenty-five cents way back when."

Julian was amazed by the stories and he thought more and more about the fabric of the neighborhood, as he traveled through with his furry four-legged friends. Julian began to see just how many new faces there were in the neighborhood and it seemed like he was slowly becoming an outsider. Maybe it had been happening longer than he realized, he just hadn't noticed. He wondered where Mrs. Chavez would go if she got forced out of her home.

He didn't know where he fit in or where he felt at home anymore, without Nana's presence and the fact that the neighborhood was becoming increasingly unfamiliar by the day. Since he had been cleaning up the old house, he began to convert the garage into a studio where he could paint. He finally decided that it was time to paint again. He loved to crank up his alternative rock music and get lost in his world of paint. A few curious neighbors would occasionally stop and watch the artist create. Julian didn't mind and was happy that anyone took notice of his work. He hadn't painted since declining the scholarships and dealing with the passing of Nana Ofelia. He had hoped to gain new inspiration, and building the studio was his first step in doing so. The studio was incredible, he hung his paintings all around, the space began to tell its own story. He also hung up some poems next to the paintings. After a few weeks, he invited more people in, to visit the space. Most of the visitors were the new transplants in the neighborhood. He wondered why the old neighbors hadn't come in to the studio. Could it have been that they also felt disenfranchised?

He could sense that the old neighbors didn't like how the neighborhood was changing. How could he bring the old and new to common ground, he wondered? Julian continued his dog walking, which actually became pretty therapeutic for him. The dogs gave him a sense of purpose and he took pride in being the best walker in the area. It was nearly impossible for people not to notice Julian, you could see him running down the block with numerous dogs; the dogs put an ear to ear smile on his face. People could see that he enjoyed what he did for a living, he was peculiar yet intriguing. Out of habit he still walked around the neighborhood, even though he had no dogs. He had a new-found joy and it was contagious. He began speaking to people and the new neighbors were curious to know him. He could hold an intellectual conversation with the best of them. It was hard not to take notice that the young charismatic man was unique.

Sully, was a local man who frequented the park benches, sometimes taking a nap or having a full-blown conversation with himself on any given day. Julian had known of the man for years and was frightened by the man's outbursts that he witnessed growing up. Everyone thought that Sully was just a crazy old drunk, as did Julian. One bright Sunday afternoon, Julian decided to sit and talk with Sully. Maybe the man wasn't crazy at all and he wanted to find out for himself.

"May I have a seat?" Julian asked.

"Of course, young man, step into my office." Julian could smell the whiskey on the man's breath as he drew closer.

"Tell me your story and I'll tell you mine," Sully said with a serious look on his face, as he put on a broken pair of bifocals.

Julian was caught off guard by the question. What did the man want to know, he wondered? Sully could see that Julian looked perplexed by the question.

"I can see that you have no story yet," Sully subtly laughed, with his legs sophistically crossed. Julian looked at Sully, dumbfounded by his rude remark. "Young man, we all have a story, we just have to learn how to share our stories with others." Sully uncrossed his legs and took another swig of the bottle he had under his sweater. Julian could smell that the man hadn't taken a shower in a while. Sully offered out his right hand and with the bottle wrapped tight around his dirty hand asked, "Do you want a drink?" At first Julian didn't respond, as he didn't know how he should proceed. He thought that it would be rude not to accept a drink of the bottle, and that the man had probably gone through a lot of trouble to get it. And so, he reluctantly grabbed the bottle and took a long swig.

As the alcohol burned down Julian's throat, Sully proceeded, "You see young man, I have a million lifetimes of stories, these things don't happen overnight." "Your story is part of who you are, and part who you want to be; part past and part present." Julian had not yet spoken a word to Sully, he just listened to the drunk old man speak. Julian immediately felt a little drunk himself, as he wasn't a drinker. He wasn't sure if the alcohol intensified the conversation, but he was suddenly intrigued by what Sully was saying. "You see son, we either become who we are meant to be, or we spend our lives fighting who we know we are to be." "*Me*, I'm meant to be a storyteller; there are many storytellers amongst us, they come in all different forms and are found in common and uncommon places." "Look, most people avoid me, because I sit on this bench day after day with my friends Jack and Daniel." Julian realized that Sully was referring to the Jack Daniels whiskey bottle that he was holding on to dear life to. "It is hard for people to accept knowledge from a drunk." In that moment Julian saw the commonality between he and Sully.

"My nana said that I was misunderstood and now I know what she meant."

Sully took a closer look at Julian's face. "Are you Ofelia and Leo's grandson?" Sully asked as he drew closer to him. Julian was taken aback that Sully knew his grandparents; he never had the chance to meet his grandfather. His curiosity grew when he heard their names.

"Yes," he excitedly responded, they are my grandparents, I mean *were* my grandparents." Julian's face then fell to the ground.

Sully firmly lifted Julian's chin and said, "In this life we must experience pain and loss in order to test the limits of our inner strengths."

Julian lifted his head and with his eyes he said, "Thank you," to Sully.

"Your grandparents were something special alright. Everyone in this neighborhood knew them; they were a strong man and woman that people looked up to. Your grandfather was heavily involved in the community, he was loved by many."

Julian's sadness transitioned into pride as he heard how great his grandparents were, as witnessed by someone else. Nana Ofelia was never one to brag and Julian felt unaware of some of the details of her life. And just as Sully started telling him the story about how he knew the couple, he began to pass out. Julian could see he was losing Sully to Jack and Daniel and so he thought it best to leave him in peace. Julian walked back to the house, thoughts running through his mind with each and every step he took. He wished he could be transported back in time just to see the glorious people he came from.

Word was getting around the neighborhood that Julian had an art studio and was doing live paintings during the evenings. And so, several people came by to watch him paint. He previously painted serene pictures with lush gardens and beautiful mountainous landscapes. The depictions of those paintings reflected times that he felt alone; the serene images supplied a peace to his soul. He described his emotions through many poems as well. Soon people who visited the studio began buying his paintings and he didn't mind the extra money. He thought about taking his talents to the streets; maybe painting some murals. He spoke to a couple of shop owners and they agreed to the art but were very specific about the images that they wanted displayed. Julian painted a couple of murals, and even though they were beautiful, they held no real reflection of anything that moved him. Julian continued his dog walking and often saw Sully at the park. He stopped to talk to him to ask him what he thought about the new murals around the neighborhood.

"They're okay, if what you want to see is art," Sully said. Julian looked confused. "If you want to tell a story, you will have to paint something very different." Julian understood what Sully was trying to say but he didn't know exactly *how* he would tell a story. Julian thanked him for his advice and told him he would come back when he had figured something out. Sully gave him a thumbs up and continued his conversation with his friends Jack and Daniel.

The next few days Julian walked around the neighborhood talking to people about topics like, what they liked about the neighborhood, the memories they had, what hopes they had for their children growing up there. He spoke to everyone, old families and new transplants alike. He began to feel saddened for the families who had lived there for many years, as they shared their generational memories with him. He heard many stories about the history of the community. He was intrigued by stories of the old days when his grandparents were just a young man and woman living there. Life was simple, and people worked hard to give their children the best.

It was a working-class neighborhood and the people in general were very honest, hardworking people. He saw the despair in the old neighbor's eyes when they expressed fear about being pushed out. Old neighbors were being offered big money to sell out, with no-where to go. Where would they go? he thought. He was questioned by some neighbors about where he would go if he ever decided to sell the house, a question he was unable to answer. He thought about all the years of memories that would be erased and he began to hear how some people felt about the neighborhood.

"Not *all* change, is good change," Mrs. Chavez said.

He told her that he understood that people like herself, want to hold on to the good memories they have.

"Yes, I have raised my children in this neighborhood, this is home," she said.

A fire swiftly ignited in Julian's heart.

"Home is where you have planted your family roots," he said during a speech at the local school; clapping and cheering could be heard coming from the lunchroom. He was becoming a voice, an advocate for those who felt they had no longer possessed ownership of their neighborhood, the only home they had ever known. Julian was honored to speak on behalf of the old neighbors. He planned to do a huge art piece echoing the stories the people had shared with him. He thought that if he could use his art to make a difference, he was honorably going to do so. But first, he decided to take some kids from around the community, to explore the murals that were previously created around the neighborhood. He wanted to gain a perspective from them about what their translation of the art pieces were. He had done his homework before the excursion, interviewing the artists that he could locate, about their artwork.

"I can see that you're finally creating a story," Sully said, as Julian passed the park. Julian began to grasp what Sully meant.

"I'm trying to tell a story," Julian responded.

Sully gave a firm nod to the zealous young man. Julian was beginning to realize that perhaps Nana had a greater purpose for leaving him the house. Could it be that she wanted him to preserve tradition and family history that they had in the tiny yellow house? Soon, people confided in Julian about their concerns of the neighborhood. Their concerns consisted of issues such as a lack of street signage, and failing schools in the area. He helped them create solutions and spoke to elected officials about their concerns. The once misunderstood, young boy, was proudly becoming a man of vision and purpose. Sully eventually shared more stories about his grandparent's community involvement, as it turned out, his grandfather founded support groups for families of Veterans and was involved in education and equity for minority students.

"You are more like your grandparents than you realize," Sully said. "Your grandmother used to sit in this very park with you when you were an infant."

Julian imagined what his nana hoped for him to be when he grew up. He certainly believed that Nana would have big dreams for him. It wasn't enough to be an average person who worked a nine to five job. She consistently asked all her grandchildren what they were doing to change the world, rather than how their job was going. Although Julian knew her well, he didn't always understand her rationale. Julian was a genius in his own right, but he knew that Nana was far more intelligent than he could ever be.

One peaceful Saturday morning, just as Julian brewed himself a hot cup of tea in his studio, he saw a man walking towards him.

"Are you the owner of this house?" a man dressed in a tightly fitted grey Armani suit asked him.

"Yes, why?"

"My name is Dillan Miller, I am a developer, and I would like to buy this property, as is, if available."

"No man, I am not selling this property!"

Julian was offended by the inquiry, he took it personal. The house was roughly eight hundred square feet and not in the best shape, wear and tear of many years of living showed.

The man said, "Well here's my card if you reconsider, which I'm sure you will; I will make you an offer you won't be able to refuse, *in time.*"

Julian soon discovered that the area was being looked at by developers who wanted to build high priced modern townhomes. A couple of home owners on the block had already sold their places. He understood how it could be difficult to pass up the hefty offers, especially to folks who were at or below poverty level. He decided at that moment that he was not going to be forced out, and that he was going to stand firm and protect the only home he had ever known. Not only was it because of the sentimental value the house had but also because it was a matter of principle for him. He knew that the developers would come and scrape the house and erase every memory in held. *How can these millionaires think that we will sell our homes, our memories, our legacy?"* he said to himself. He found it disconcerting that his community was being torn apart right in front of his very own eyes.

As Julian sat on his front porch, he reminisced about when he was a child growing up there. He laughed to himself, as he remembered Nana chasing after him. To his surprise, she would always catch him; she would pick him up and kiss him all over his face, he could smell her perfume. She spun him around until he became dizzy, but he loved it. Maybe he didn't run as fast as he could have because he secretly wanted her affection. The recollections made Julian feel like he was exactly where he needed to be, *home.*

"Hello...Daisy!" Julian was thrilled to hear from his old friend, since it had been a while that they last spoke to each other. Daisy was finishing up school and she was just as thrilled to hear Julian's voice. Julian shared what he had been doing in the community and Daisy was impressed and ever so proud of him.

"I'm thinking about coming back after school," she said.

"We would love to have you back home!"

Daisy was finishing up her Political Science degree. He was convinced that if anyone could assist him in his efforts to preserve the neighborhood, it would be her. Julian found an old picture of his grandparents standing in front of the house on Sherman Street. The house looked a little different, it was before the fire that happened, years before. Julian wanted to give the picture life, and so he hung it up in the studio and captioned it with a poem:

A house isn't just a house

The walls aren't simply, walls

We preserve our memories by listening to the walls talk about when we were children

Young and innocent

Searching for a purpose

Flowers that grow in our gardens tell stories of the hard work that built our house

The house that looks like a castle, our castle

A castle where we reign as the princes of our forefathers

We are the house and our memories will forever be embedded in our walls.

Julian thought about including the picture and poem as a part of a project that he was working on. The project was a community collective, showcasing the artists, story tellers, and visionaries of the neighborhood. Julian began to discover that there were others like himself, who wanted to preserve the neighborhood's history by storytelling. He was definitely in good company and learned to surround himself with likeminded people; Julian was teachable and determined to make a difference.

"Sully, can you come to the event I'm having?" "I would like you to speak, because you know a lot about the history of the neighborhood."

"I'm sorry, young man, but nobody wants to hear from someone like me. I share my stories in my office, on this bench with my friends, Jack and Daniel. I am where I am supposed to be. I don't need a platform to tell my stories. You on the other hand are meant to be on a platform. Your grandmother left you more than just that house."

Julian was disappointed that one of the most intelligent men he knew, declined his request, but nonetheless he respected his position. Julian wanted his support but realized that perhaps the man had taken him as far as he could on this journey. The kids in the neighborhood were curious about Julian's artwork and soon he started a class for the youth out of his studio. Their work would also be included in the show. Julian was very excited for the special event.

A week before the show, Daisy called to announce her return to Colorado. He was thrilled that he would have another likeminded person on his side. To his surprise she told him of her intentions to run for a City Council seat. "Wow, I think that's a great idea Daisy." "You will be able to help me with the work I am doing to preserve the neighborhood." Julian could hear a shift in Daisy's voice and quickly picked up that perhaps she no longer shared the same ideology.

"I understand what you are trying to do Julian, but you have to understand that neighborhoods need to change in order to evolve."

Suddenly, he wasn't so excited to meet the new Daisy. He felt disappointed and betrayed that she had changed so much that she no longer understood him, as she previously had.

"It seems that you have learned a lot in college, Daisy. I've learned a lot here too, and I know that my eyes and my ears have not betrayed me; and the way I now view things hold many truths."

After an awkward moment of silence, the two exchanged a brief good bye and hung up.

That evening Julian could not sleep, he was perturbed by the new, educated, disconnected, Daisy. The fact that someone could change like that, caused him great disappointment; which seemed to happen overnight. Perhaps he didn't pick up on her subtle hints over the many conversations they had, while she was away at college. He struggled with the fact that someone could just become someone else so quickly. What happens to people, people who forget where they come from? Could such change be motivated by money, or a false sense of power? All these things really made Julian feel saddened. He went to see Sully the next morning to share the occurrence. As soon as Julian could see Sully in direct view, he noticed that he was not in the company of his friends Jack and Daniel. It seemed strange, as he was never without his friends.

"Are you ok Sully?"

"Yes, boy, why do you ask?"

Julian didn't want to offend him therefore, he didn't pry. He noticed that Sully looked cleaned up, which wasn't a bad thing. Julian told Sully about Daisy and how he felt betrayed by one of the last people he trusted.

"My young man, these things happen, life isn't easy, and you will face much opposition when you try to do the right thing." "Unfortunately, opposition may come from people that we thought we knew."

"But she was my friend, Sully!" Sully could see that Julian was very upset, nearly to the point of tears.

"Young man, life is full of disappointments, we only have the power to be the person who doesn't disappoint others."

Julian thanked Sully for listening, he had really become someone that he valued. Julian even felt bad about how he had previously viewed the man before getting to know him. Soon after the conversation between Julian and Daisy occurred, her grandmother, Mrs. Chavez told him that Daisy was coming home to fix the neighborhood. Since Julian knew of Daisey's intentions, he had to think of a strategy, since she would be returning soon. He now knew that she would be working against him and his efforts.

Meanwhile, Julian kept working on the neighborhood collective. He included old artists, new artists, the children who attended his classes, and other artists in the celebration. It was an exciting night and a diverse gathering. Julian was pleased with how many people were in attendance. And to his surprise, some of his family members attended, including Uncle Hector. The displayed artwork reflected the neighborhood old and new. Poets and musicians colorfully displayed their talents, like the paintings on the wall.

The most highly anticipated portion of the evening would be the unveiling of the mural that Julian painted in the park. He had been mindfully gathering images from the conversations he had with people in the neighborhood; he also gathered ideas from his students. The piece was such a unique depiction of the story he wanted to tell. It was a story of old traditions and new ideas, a story of a family's perseverance and their hope for a better future. It was the story of his grandparents and the story of Sully. He even included Daisy and himself as young kids exploring the neighborhood on bicycles. The mural included the shoe store on the corner and the yellow house on Sherman Street.

Lastly, the mural included the park bench, where he learned from a great man about his own history. The park bench where he envisioned himself sitting on his Nana Ofelia's lap, as she planted her hopes for his future. Julian finally had a story to tell and he promised himself to share as much of his story and the history that lied within the neighborhood, to everyone. He vowed to represent the hopeless and defend the honor of the people who came before.

Julian learned that home lies within a person's soul, a moment in time, and in the place where our roots are planted. And whether we choose to leave or stay, we can never erase the memories that lie within. He learned that sometimes friends become family and that sometimes certain people can only stay in our lives for a while. He decided that he would forever remain in the small yellow house. He believed that's what Nana wanted, and that she entrusted him to fulfill her wishes for his life. He vowed to raise his own children there and to teach them everything he knew about how they could create their own story. He vowed to continue the fight for promoting a harmonious community where the old and the new could not only co-exist but thrive. He noticed that Daisy was at the event and at the end of the evening, she approached him.

"Thank you for telling your story through the mural Julian," she said. "I needed to see and hear that story. Sometimes people, including myself need to be reminded of where we come from. I suppose, I fell out of touch; I can't promise you that we will always see eye to eye or that we will be fighting for the same things. But I can promise you that I will always remember the things that I have learned here tonight."

Julian hoped that what he had given to Daisy and to the people that night, would be enough to have a positive impact in the community for years to come. He hoped that someday, his own story would be told. He somehow finally felt understood; so much in fact, that he decided to make a run at a City Council seat, where he defeated his opponent *Daisy Chavez*.

CHAPTER FIVE

Cooking Up Hope

"YOU SHOULD ALWAYS BELIEVE THAT SOMETHING GOOD WILL HAP-
PEN," FIVE-YEAR-OLD LENA TOLD HER MOTHER CLARISSA, AS THEY SAT
IN THEIR OLD, HAND ME DOWN HONDA. Clarissa was moved to tears
at what her daughter said and was thankful to her for the hopeful
reminder. Clarissa was in her mid-twenties, now a single mother
to Lena. She had been married since she was eighteen, to her high
school sweetheart, Ben. She once loved him, but over time his true
colors began to show. Ben became extremely verbally abusive and
had controlling behavior. He had Clarissa right where he wanted her
and after a few years of the abuse, she finally conjured up the strength
to leave him. She wondered how she even came to be involved in
such a tumultuous relationship.

Ultimately, she knew that she wanted better for her daughter
and would do anything to prevent her from further being exposed
to abuse. She felt regret for exposing her, for as long as she had.
Lena was growing up fast, and Clarissa knew Ben's behavior would
be even more difficult to mask. Ben hadn't always been abusive,
in fact in the presence of others, he was a charmer, and very well

liked. Clarissa would be the only one to feel his wrath; he kept his abusive behavior hidden from others. A part of Clarissa died during the years she spent with him. Her departure surely caused her to be braver than ever before. Although brave, she was unsure how she could adequately provide for Lena. But anytime doubt entered her mind, she focused on Lena's smile. She never wanted to see her smile fade, as her own did, during the years spent in the marriage. With nowhere to go, they left with only a few duffle bags in tow.

Clarissa worked at a laundromat and did everything she could to provide for her daughter, but the little money she earned never seemed to be enough. Many days Clarissa didn't have enough money to eat, but she didn't care as long as Lena ate and had everything she needed.

She was fortunate to be able to bring Lena to work with her; her boss Mr. Nguyen was an understanding man. The long hours made it seem like they lived there. Mr. Nguyen tried to give her as many extra hours as he possibly could, without it being noticeable by his wife, who managed the books. Mrs. Nguyen was not as friendly to Clarissa, but she did treat Lena fairly well. Mr. Nguyen did his best to help Clarissa, since he knew that she had some pretty rough days. He didn't know the specifics of her life but could see the sadness in her eyes.

Lena was a sweet child, with eyes as bright as stars on a clear night. She was such an innocent and loving soul. She didn't understand everything she and her mom went through, she was less concerned with their circumstances and more concerned with her mother leaving her. "I will never leave you", Clarissa reassured her, daily. And as her mother spoke those reaffirming words to her, she sighed in relief and was comforted again.

Ben was a spiteful man; he didn't care what happened to Clarissa or Lena, after they escaped. Even though Clarissa tried to hide a lot of the abuse from Lena, the young girl would overhear her dad saying things like, "You know you're not very smart", to her mom.

"You won't ever find anyone to love you, like I do," he said a lot of hateful things. In addition to being abusive, he was a womanizer. Clarissa discovered that he had another woman in is life, who was pregnant with child. She knew that he would be preoccupied with his new family and too busy for Lena. He would need all his time and energy, to mold his new woman into what he wanted her to be. In a way, Clarissa was glad that he would be preoccupied because he would have less time, to torment them. Lena didn't seem to mind that her father wasn't in their lives anymore. She knew, even at that young age, that he made her mom sad. Clarissa knew that children are smarter than what adults give them credit for. She felt disappointed at the way her life was going. She thought it was unfair and knew it wasn't supposed to be the way that it was turning out. Nonetheless, being in her predicament angered her to the point that she used the anger as motivation to do better. She was determined to make it on her own, without the help of a man. Clarissa's cell phone rang and as the ringtone of *What a Wonderful World,* played, she could see that it was Nana Ofelia calling.

"Hello?"

"Hi mija, it's Nana."

"Hi Nana, how are you?"

Nana somehow knew the right times to call Clarissa. "I made dinner mija, you and your family are welcomed to come over to eat." Clarissa had been showing up at Nana's with just Lena, since she left Ben. She didn't want to worry Nana with her issues and was very selective about what she shared with her. Nana admired Clarissa, she reminded her a lot of herself. Besides the fact that they were a splitting image of each other, with green eyes and full lips, they also shared a lot of the same passions.

Their love for all things domestic, kept them close. Clarissa learned how to cook and sew from Nana. A couple of times a week the two of them shared a few cups of coffee in the kitchen, while Nana coached Clarissa through some recipes. Clarissa loved the time they spent together, and she learned some valuable lessons from her during the weekly interactions.

Clarissa was estranged from her mother, Martha, and had been for some time. Her mother disapproved of the marriage to Ben, especially because she was aware of the abuse. Irrespective of her mother's disapproval, Clarissa had felt a stronger bond with Nana since she was a young girl. She supposed that she felt closer to her because she never criticized her and always made her feel important. Not only had she made her feel important, but she made her believe that she was capable of being successful in life, despite obstacles. Clarissa felt that she always had to prove something to gain the approval of her mother. And her sister Fiona, an attorney, was a hard act to follow. She often wondered why her mother couldn't just love her, unconditionally, like Nana had. At times, Clarissa felt that her mother was envious of the relationship she shared with Nana but never understood why, after all, she was her mother.

"Mija, your mother just wants the best for you, that is why she is hard on you."

"I know deep down that she does Nana, but she is so hard and after so many years of her putting me down, I just can't be around her anymore."

"Oh mija, your mother has been that way since she was a child." "All of my kids are different, but they *do* love, *she* just has her own way of showing it."

At times Clarissa's mom would compare her to her sister Fiona, which led to further resentment.

"Mija, we cannot choose who are parents are, but they were chosen to bring you into the world for a reason. Whether the relationship is in good standing or not, simply extract the good in what they have shown you, even if it's just one thing. I know that one day you two will reunite, when you learn to forgive. I believe something good will happen and you should believe the same."

"You always have the right words to say Nana, one of the many reasons I love you."

Clarissa finished drying the dishes from the pots that accumulated from the delicious posole they made that brisk afternoon. Lena sat patiently at the table waiting for her great grandma to prepare the bag of goodies she sent her home with, when she visited. The goodie bags weren't small, and there were usually enough treats to last a week. Lena thanked Nana for the bag of goodies, in her soft voice. Lena's inner spirit radiated like the sun. Nana told Clarissa that Lena was a *Rainbow Child*, sent from the universe to remind people not to lose hope. As Clarissa glanced over at the excited little girl opening the bag, she was reminded of her reason to keep going every day. Lena had such an innocence, and Clarissa hoped that her daughter would never experience disappointment, as she had. Part of Clarissa believed that Lena was a Rainbow Child, just like Nana said.

Nana had become old and fragile, but somehow had the strength to lift Lena up, onto her waist, she then smothered her with enough hugs to last a lifetime. Clarissa remembered the same embrace by Nana when she was a little girl. Clarissa never took for granted the fact that Lena was blessed to have even met her great grandmother, and moreover was blessed, to experience her love firsthand.

Since Clarissa had recently left Ben, she hadn't yet saved enough money to get a place. Housing in Denver was expensive and required deposits that would take her at least a few months to save for. Her sister Fiona offered for her to come and stay with her, in Chicago. She considered the offer but decided to stay put for a while. Since she couldn't afford a place of her own, she decided that they would sleep in the car until they could get a place. No one knew the totality of the circumstances and Clarissa would make sure that it stayed that way. As she placed blankets in the back seat of the car, she made it as comfortable as possible for Lena. She strategically placed stuffed animals to surround Lena; she promised her that the stuffed animals would keep her safe at night. The sunroof in the car served as a Segway to the stars, that Clarissa wished upon nightly.

"Mommy, what do *you* ask the stars for tonight?" Lena asked.

"I wish that when you grow up, you will be surrounded by the best people the universe has."

"Isn't everyone nice mommy?"

"Well baby, everyone is born good."

"Why wouldn't they stay good forever?" she curiously asked.

Frankly, Clarissa didn't have the answers to every question her daughter asked. She became perplexed at times and withheld certain things from her as she didn't want Lena to know too much about life, especially the unpleasant things.

Clarissa's tears had a regular appointment with the darkness, that arrived at night. She tried her best not to let her baby girl see her cry. The despair that clouded her mind is something she thought may never leave. Every time she seemed to take a step forward, something happened that caused her to take ten steps backward.

One Friday evening, Clarissa was folding the last load of laundry for Mr. Moore, a local businessman. She would be closing up the laundromat soon. Lena sat at the table watching her favorite cartoon and Clarissa could see that she was tired, as she yawned every couple of minutes. It was payday and Mr. Nguyen allowed Clarissa to have an extra few minutes on her break to go and cash her check earlier that morning. Clarissa placed her money in her small backpack that she stored in her locker. Towards the end of her shift, she grabbed her backpack and brought it up to the counter. She thought it would be safe there as there was no one else in the laundromat. Just as she began to turn off the lights, starting in the back room, she saw a teenaged boy running out of the laundromat with her backpack in tow. Clarissa's heart was beating out of her chest, as she ran out to catch the boy. To no avail, she gave up after about a block. The adrenaline caused tunnel vision and as she snapped out of it, she ran back to her daughter. As Clarissa ran back to the laundromat, she could see Lena looking out the door, curious as to why she had been running, and yelling "Stop!" What would she tell her baby girl about the good people who do bad things?

That night Lena cried tears until they dried up like the Arizona desert. And she wondered how she would feed her daughter that week. Clarissa wouldn't ask anyone for anything, not out of pride but more so because she didn't want to be viewed as a failure. Or even worse, have someone call the authorities on her for being an unfit mother. The theft would set her back another couple of weeks, which meant that the two of them would have to sleep in the car a while longer. Clarissa was worried about the cold and snow that would soon be headed their way. *There has to be a better life*, Clarissa thought. She didn't attend college after high school because she wanted to be a stay-at- home mom, like women were in the past. She was more traditional in her thinking and willingly took on the role; she never expected to be in the predicament that she found herself in. To make matters worse, just when Clarissa thought Ben went away, he resurfaced. He wanted to make her miserable, after his new woman left him. He was now focused on finding a way to get back at her for leaving him, and he did just that.

Clarissa and Lena went to see Nana for their weekly cooking lesson. "Ben stopped by the other day," Nana said. Clarissa's immediately felt a lump in the back of her throat. She didn't want Nana to worry and she knew that she would become worrisome for her, if she thought they were in danger. "I know that you left him, and I *also* know why."

"You do?" Clarissa asked.

"Of course, I have seen the hurt in your eyes for a long while now. I have witnessed many situations during my lifetime and can recognize them, especially when my own family is experiencing them, it's called intuition and life experience mija."

Clarissa didn't know what to say and there was an awkward silence. She thought that for the first time in her life, Nana might be disappointed in her. Clarissa was furious that Ben told Nana what had happened. Nana began cooking some arroz con leche, rice pudding. And then she defensively said, "I told Ben that I was happy that you left," while waving her wooden spatula in the air. Clarissa swiftly lifted her head up, surprised not only by what Nana said but how she said it.

"I told him that you cannot keep a wounded bird down forever. You see Clarissa, birds were created to fly, and they eventually find a way back to doing what they were created to do. I commend you for your bravery and I will always support your decisions. You will know what you are to do, when you listen to your heart, trust yourself and favor will be yours."

Clarissa cried on Nana's shoulder and she made her feel like she was more than capable of doing something great with her life. Clarissa didn't tell her about her living situation, but she had a feeling that intuition told the story.

That evening the wind and rain were howling. It was hard to sleep as the car swayed to and fro with the wind currents. Lena was scared of the lightening and Clarissa did her best to comfort her, by holding her tight; neither of them could sleep. Clarissa turned the radio up loud to drown out the noise, Lena loved to listen to jazz. She liked the fact that there were no words and that she could make up her own.

"Mom why does it rain anyway?" Lena asked.

"I think that maybe God is crying." "Sometimes because He's sad and sometimes because He's happy." Lena looked amazed by what she had learned.

"Is He sad about the nice people who do bad things?"

"Maybe…but maybe He is sad because he created people to be special and they don't believe they are special."

Clarissa wondered if she was as curious as Lena as a child and thought about how her mother would answer such questions. She knew that eventually Lena would grow and see the world for what it really was, and the thought scared her. Clarissa didn't want Lena to ever grow up.

"If only we could keep our children young forever," Nana said. "That's why it is so important to capture and cherish the tiny moments in life."

"I understand Nana, I am trying to raise a child who will be well equipped for the world."

"You know it's okay to be a realist mija but it's also equally important to be a dreamer. I had many dreams throughout my life, I suppose dreaming of things I couldn't experience kept me curious. Curiosity has always been by my side."

Clarissa had dreams of her own. She foremost dreamt of being a great mother and wife. She had envisioned herself seeing Lena off to school and then spending the rest of the day taking care of her home and making a delicious dinner for her daughter and husband. Clarissa was infatuated with the idea of the traditional family unit. She was heartbroken that things were not turning out as she had envisioned.

"Mija, some things in life are meant to be planned and some are not. Sometimes the unplanned take us to places we wouldn't otherwise travel to. The universe moves in a way that takes you to where you should be at the right time."

Nana Ofelia was full of wisdom and sound advice. But she also allowed her grandchildren to experience the things they needed to experience. As weeks went on, Clarissa was certain that Nana knew about them living in the car. And she wondered why she hadn't asked about it or offer to help them. Ultimately, she knew that there must have been good reason. Lena would sometimes mention the car and describe the magical conversations that happened in the car, moments between she and her mom.

As Clarissa crossed the street over to the laundromat, holding Lena's hand tightly, she noticed that the restaurant next door to the laundromat had a *For Lease* sign hanging from the window.

The restaurant wasn't doing very well, and in fact it was the second restaurant to fail at that location in three short years. Clarissa thought about how difficult managing a restaurant must be. The restaurant seemed to have all the right things going for it; fancy décor and wait staff that mirrored models. The model-like waiters carried trays of food and wine bottles with the elegance of figure skaters. She felt bad for the failed restaurant that she could never afford to eat in.

"Mr. Nguyen, what happened to the restaurant?"

"You know these trendy, overpriced restaurants can't survive in this neighborhood." "Well, that's too bad, Clarissa said."

That night as Clarissa held Lena tight, she glared out into the stars. Clarissa imagined that by some miracle, she might have her own restaurant one day. After all, Nana said it was good to have dreams. She would teach her daughter to dream, big, impossible, ridiculous dreams. That night something changed, and Clarissa felt that the universe would show her favor. She knew that someday she would get a chance to show the world that she was capable of being someone other than who she currently was.

Clarissa decided to devise a plan towards accomplishing her dreams, as she was fully aware that dreams require action. She told Mr. Nguyen that she would work through the end of the year, and then she would be leaving to work in a restaurant. Mr. Nguyen supported her decision and wasn't upset like she expected him to be. He had been a good boss and she was the only non-related employee. She was a hard worker, someone he could truly depend on. He equally liked Lena and enjoyed having the little ray of sunshine at the laundromat. He also made it as comfortable as he could for her. "Thank you for your understanding Mr. Nguyen, you are a nice man." Mr. Nguyen cracked a slight grin as he walked away from her to collect the coins from the machines.

"My mom is going to be a Chef!" Lena told Nana.

Clarissa than had no choice but to share her dreams with her.

"Nana, I want to cook like you do and share the food with

everyone." Nana was flattered by what she said. "May I start writing your recipes down, so I won't forget anything?"

"Mija, you see how I cook, a splash of this and a dash of that."

"But everything is so delicious," Clarissa said.

"Food is a gift from Mother Earth and was created to be shared, not only is it nourishment for our bodies but it's intended to fill our souls." "How many memories do you have that were created over food?" Nana asked.

Clarissa remembered family gatherings where food was the centerpiece, and everyone shared in the moment, truly enjoying one another's company. She remembered the many conversations that took place in that kitchen with Nana, over a meal.

A few months later, Clarissa had enough money to get a place of her own. She began apartment hunting, but everything was out of her budget. She was scared to commit to something she wasn't sure she could afford. "Your clothes are ready to go Mr. Moore." Clarissa quickly jumped off the torn-up chair where she was sitting, while having dinner with Lena. Clarissa had pulled out a plastic table cloth, lit a candle, and placed a vase with artificial flowers at the table in the laundromat. Mr. Moore was the best dressed man that Clarissa had ever seen. He wore stylish hats and custom suits with shining shoes. He drove a white Mercedes-Benz and had a few other high-end cars that he switched back and forth from. Clarissa had never really had a conversation with Mr. Moore, besides small talk. Clarissa quickly grabbed his order as he looked at her with an impatient glare.

"Here you go, you're all set." Clarissa noticed that Mr. Moore looked a little tired, more than usual.

"Are you doing ok Mr. Moore?"

"I had a long week closing on the property I bought."

"Oh, I see, well I hope you get some much-needed rest, she said."

Mr. Moore continued talking, which he had not done before. She supposed he just needed a listening ear, and she happily obliged.

"I purchased the restaurant next door," he said.

"I was wondering what happened, as I saw the sign on the door," Clarissa said.

"I am planning to reopen it as a new restaurant, I just want to get the right renters in there." She continued to listen to him.

"Well, good luck Mr. Moore, I know you will be successful in whatever you do."

"Thank you, young lady."

Clarissa began looking for work at various restaurants around the neighborhood. She hadn't yet been offered a job, so she continued working at the laundromat. Over the next couple of weeks, she saw Mr. Moore at the restaurant. He was doing a complete overhaul of the place. It looked beautiful, from what she could see when the workers left the doors ajar.

Clarissa and Lena had plans with Nana early that Saturday morning, but the cooking session was brief because Clarissa had to work that afternoon. Clarissa packed up the calabacita, squash, corn soup that they had prepared, to be consumed later at work. It was a busy afternoon at the laundromat, as most Saturdays were. It was so busy that Clarissa hadn't even a few minutes to eat. She figured she had better feed Lena, as Lena kept munching on the bag of old pretzels that Mr. Nguyen gave her. And so, she warmed the soup up for her. Lena set up the table on her own that afternoon. Just as Lena blew on a spoonful of soup and began to take her first bite, Mr. Moore came in to pick up his laundry. Clarissa was finishing folding his last load. When Lena saw him, she waved him over to her and invited him to have a seat at her makeshift dinner table.

"You can have a lunch with me, while you wait Mr. Moore." How could he resist such a sincere offer from the tiny girl?

"What are you having for lunch?" Before she could answer he continued, "It smells divine."

Lena ran to the break room, pulled the wooden stool towards the cabinets and grabbed a bowl and spoon for him.

"My nana and my mom made this soup this morning, I helped them," she proudly proclaimed. Mr. Moore helped himself to the soup as he hadn't had lunch yet, or breakfast for that matter.

"This is excellent soup young lady, possibly the best I've ever tasted."

"Thank you," she proudly replied. "My mom loves to cook, and she is going to be a chef."

"Oh, *is* she?"

Mr. Moore played along, realizing that kids tend to be imaginative. As he took his last bite of soup, Clarissa shouted out, "All done Mr. Moore!" When he didn't answer, she curiously glanced around and finally saw that he was sitting over by Lena. She quickly ran over to see what her baby girl was saying to the man.

"Your laundry is ready Mr. Moore."

He looked at her and asked, "Did you make that wonderful soup I just devoured?"

"Yes Mr. Moore, that is one of my grandmother's signature dishes, she has taught me everything I know about cooking."

"Well, that was pretty darn delish, and your little girl was kind enough to share it with me."

"You are welcomed to eat here whenever we have food," Clarissa said. "I usually cook with my grandmother a couple of times a week." "If you're next door, I'll send Lena over to get you or we can send the food over."

"I would love to taste more," he said with an ear to ear grin.

"Perfect," she said.

Lena jumped out of her chair and surprised the man with a hug, bigger than herself. Lena seemed to like him, and Clarissa felt relieved that her daughter didn't have a negative view of men. Over the next few months, Clarissa kept her word and fed him a couple of times a week. He sampled many wonderful dishes that she prepared and was taking note of all the food. He thought that he would love to feature some of the savory dishes at the new restaurant.

Clarissa often talked to Nana, about Mr. Moore. Nana jokingly expressed that she was flattered that the man enjoyed their cooking, even though she knew that she was the best cook around. She didn't mind sending extras when they cooked. Clarissa loved the cooking sessions with Nana, and equally loved the stories that came along with the sessions.

Nana Ofelia held up two onions and said, "You see these onions mija, when I was a little girl, I would have to pick these, one by one alongside my father." "We worked for what seemed like an eternity; the work was without end." Nana continued to chop the onions for the stew that they were making that morning.

"I suppose I never realized how hard my tiny hands were working. I just enjoyed being with my dad and that's all I cared about at the time, he made it fun for me. He would recite silly riddles, while chasing me through the fields. He taught me how to work hard but he also taught me that there would be a reward at the end. Just as it got dark, we would fill up the trucks with crates of onions. We then brought a few of them home to my mother. She cooked her heart out and I felt proud that I contributed to the family meal."

Nana shared a story with every meal and Clarissa attentively listened; the stories made cooking more exciting. Everything was done with such precision and love. Clarissa appreciated Nana more as she was maturing as a young woman, especially because of the tumultuous relationship she had with her mother. More than ever, she needed a womanly figure in her life. She could never make sense of how her mother was so different than Nana. Clarissa wrapped up the last bag of food and said her good byes to Nana. Lena ran back to grab her goodie bag, that she forgot on the table. Clarissa loved to see how little things made her daughter smile. She considered herself blessed to be raising such a bright young girl.

"Mr. Moore, we have dinner today," Lena yelled into the opened door at the restaurant. "I'll be right over," he gladly said.

He enjoyed their meals so much, that he often skipped fancy

dinner parties that he had been invited to. That evening, Clarissa couldn't sit and have dinner. The laundromat was busy, and Mr. Nguyen was on vacation, therefore she was responsible for everything. She didn't want to overlook even the smallest detail that could result in disappointing the boss. Mr. Moore sat with Lena and they watched an episode of Seinfeld on the old television above the soda pop machine. Lena loved episodes of Seinfeld for some reason, as did Mr. Moore. The meal was more delicious and filling than the last, so much in fact that it made Mr. Moore sleepy. Lena was so comfortable with Mr. Moore, that she began telling him about their living arrangement. At first, he thought perhaps she was using her imaginative mind, as she talked about how her stuffed animals protect her in the back seat and how they wish upon the stars through the sunroof at night.

"Finish up Lena," Clarissa yelled over the row of washers. "I hope you enjoyed the food Mr. Moore," Clarissa said as she walked passed the washing machines.

"*Always,*" he replied. "I've decided that I am going to start paying you for the food."

"You don't have to do that Mr. Moore, if we have extra, we are more than happy to share. My nana taught me that if you give, even if it's something small, you will never be without. I believe it, and that's why I am happy to share what little we have."

"I will pay you," he sternly said. "You can put the money away and use it to buy the ingredients you need to prepare the food, very few things in life are free."

Lena interjected by saying, "Nana says that love is free."

Mr. Moore felt bad that the little girl overheard him making such a harsh statement. At that moment he realized just how intelligent and honest she was, and then it dawned on him that she wasn't making up the story regarding their living arrangement. As he pulled out a crisp one-hundred-dollar bill, he had an idea.

There was an apartment on top of the restaurant that was

vacant. He planned to rent it out once the restaurant was completed. Over the next couple of weeks, he hired a few guys to renovate the space. It was small, but he knew it would be adequate for Clarissa and Lena. He wanted it to be done quickly and so he hired a few more guys to expedite the project and hired an interior decorator to help furnish the apartment. After the apartment was completed to his satisfaction, he went down to the laundromat to get the girls to show them what he had done.

"Mr. Nguyen, I'll be right back." Clarissa grabbed Lena's hand and then quickly ran out of the laundromat.

"I have a proposition," Mr. Moore said. Clarissa raised her suspicious brow; the word proposition didn't sit well with her. He saw her reaction and quickly said, "If you cook for me daily, I will rent the apartment to you." Clarissa was caught off guard by the generous offer.

"I would love that," she said. "But I'm not sure I can afford the rent."

"Let me be clear, I will take food in exchange for the rent."

Lena didn't understand the details regarding the exchange but understood that they now had a place to call home. She began jumping up and down and hugged her mom's leg. "Hold on, hold on," Clarissa told her. "Mr. Moore, I can't accept this."

"Clarissa, I am a businessman, I work with numbers and I'm an expert at return on investments. I am confident that this arrangement will be a return on investment for me. You continue to feed me, and I'll be a happy man. The place is empty anyhow, and I don't need the rental income, so we will both benefit from this proposition."

Clarissa finally agreed to see the space; she and Lena were in awe by what they saw.

Indeed, it was fully furnished and had a few other quirky surprises. The décor was eclectic yet feminine at the same time. Lena ran over and jumped on the bed, surrounded by new stuffed animals. And not just any standard sized stuffed animals, huge stuffed animals that nearly engulfed the entire bed. There was custom made skylights over each of their beds, so they could see the stars at night. There was custom writing on the wall that read, *Dream the Impossible*. Mr. Moore made sure that the kitchen was filled with all the essential tools that any chef would have in their home. The final surprise was a custom designed pull-down wall table. Beside the table there was a basket filled with fancy linen and table settings that Lena could interchange; she loved acting like a waitress. It was amazing, and the girls beamed, full of joy at their new place; they moved in immediately and spent that night there.

Clarissa was overflowing with a heart of gratitude, and that night her tears were that of happiness. They quickly settled in to their new place and things finally seemed to be going well for them. Lena loved the place so much that she never wanted to leave. Mr. Moore continued to stop by for lunches or dinners; he turned out to be a kind man, which Clarissa didn't expect.

The year was coming to an end, and Clarissa finally gave her two-week notice at the laundromat. She was offered a job at a restaurant a few blocks away. She had been hired as a dishwasher, not exactly what she wanted but she was willing to start somewhere. Mr. Nguyen was sad to see her go but he was reassured that he would see them often, as they now lived next door. Mr. Moore had finally got the restaurant going after the remodel. It was another trendy restaurant, like numerous others in the neighborhood. He invited Clarissa and Lena to a soft opening they had, where she thought that the food was decent. The atmosphere was a little too formal for her liking, but she didn't let him know that. After all, he had been generous beyond measure to them over the past few months.

Clarissa was on her way to her new job, for her first day, when Mr. Moore knocked on her door.

"Hello Mr. Moore!" He could see her dressed in her new uniform and hated to bother her.

"My head chef is sick today, he called in at the last minute."

"I'm sorry to hear that but I have to go, or I will be late."

"I mean, how he could do this to me, knowing that I have some very important people coming to the restaurant tonight!" "It's Chef's Special tonight." Clarissa wondered why he was telling her all of this. She surely wasn't qualified to help him in his predicament. "Do you think you can help me, just for tonight?" he asked.

"Help you do what?" she reluctantly asked.

"Cook of course, it's chef's choice, which means you are free to create any dish you choose."

Clarissa was in shock at what Mr. Moore was asking. At that moment she was filled with doubt that she could pull something like that off. But she also felt indebted to the man for giving her so much. She began to ask him questions about how she could actually pull it off. He gave her free reign over the kitchen and unlimited access to the sous chef and other kitchen staff. He reassured her that she wouldn't be alone, she would have every tool she needed to succeed. She knew they were pressed for time and so she quickly ran downstairs to the kitchen, where she felt overwhelmed but decided to give it an honest effort. Lena ran down with her mother and quickly made friends with the wait staff.

That evening Clarissa cooked her heart out. All the love she had in her heart for her daughter, was poured into the meal. To her surprise, the meal was a hit with the customers. And that night, they weren't just any customers, they were food critics from local media outlets, which she wasn't aware of. At evenings end, it was customary for the chef to come and greet the guests. Mr. Moore called Clarissa from out of the kitchen and patted her on the shoulder as if to say, *well done*. She felt a sense of real accomplishment that night that made her believe that she could actually be a chef someday. Mr. Moore was so grateful for Clarissa and later offered her a job in the kitchen, as a special assistant to the Executive Chef. She happily accepted his offer. She realized just how much he believed in her and that motivated her to work as hard as she could.

The restaurant won Best New Restaurant of the Year, and Mr. Moore attributed the recognition to the first evening that she cooked there. He was delighted, and he knew that he needed to keep her at the restaurant; he was right about his return on investment. *"Who is Clarissa Gallegos?"* the headline of the local newspaper read. There was a favorable article written up about her and she was very proud of herself, for not losing hope in chasing her dreams. Nana was even more proud, she said that she looked like a younger version of herself in the newspaper photo. She wondered how she ended up in such a fortunate situation, and realized that things can turn around, if you don't lose hope.

As she read the article aloud to Nana, she finally believed that dreams come true, something that she would always teach her daughter. Clarissa became the Executive Chef after only nine months of working at the restaurant. She was quickly becoming one of the best young chefs in the city. She worked at Mr. Moore's restaurant for a couple of years. The job was going well, and she eventually created a menu with her own signature dishes. Everything was going well during her first two years, except that Nana Ofelia had passed. A year after she passed away, Clarissa received a package in the mail. As she curiously opened the package, she found a brown leather journal filled with hand written recipes. She recognized the handwriting, they were recipes written by Nana. On the first page there was a hand-written note that read: *YOU SHOULD ALWAYS BELIEVE THAT SOMETHING GOOD WILL HAPPEN.* Clarissa was amazed by the gift that arrived a year after Nana passed and she wondered how it was possible.

That evening, it was pouring rain outside, as the restaurant closed. Lena was standing at the door and she said, "God must be happy mom." Clarissa grabbed her daughter and took her to the rain, where they danced under happy tears that night. Clarissa and her baby girl were the happiest that they had ever been, in that moment. Clarissa was reassured that good things would continue to happen and because of her genuine love of cooking, she knew that Nana would forever be with her.

CHAPTER SIX

Truth Revealed

I don't know what I believe anymore, Analise wrote in her letter to Nana Ofelia. *I mean, if God is real, then, why does He allow such suffering in the world?* She knew that she couldn't be the only one to feel such ambivalence. She was certain that others must have questioned *why* they believed what they believed. Analise stayed in regular contact with Nana through letters and occasional phone calls. Visits with Nana, a couple of times a year, were very important to the both of them. She found it difficult to step away from work; she could be a bit controlling and didn't trust that anyone could perform her duties to her standards. Even when she was on vacation, she rarely put her phone down; she was consumed by calls and emails.

Analise had a big heart since she was a young girl, a genuine compassion for people. She began her humanitarian work as a college student, while studying abroad in various countries. She fell in love with the work, and after college went to work full time for a global nonprofit disaster organization. She was approaching her fifteenth year in the field and had become the Director of Planning. Her position, unlike other leadership positions, required her to be out in the field most of the time, assessing efficiencies. She had been to every corner of the world; and she was very good at her job. She also trained other organizations on disaster relief, everyone in the relief community knew of her work.

She had even been offered a position with FEMA but declined the offer because she preferred lending her talents to the worldwide community, rather than at the national level. She loved the United States, but she had a greater love of helping people, in poverty-stricken countries. She thought the people were more appreciative of their work and she learned new skills that she could use on a broader spectrum, from the foreign lands she worked in. She was surrounded by an amazing staff and it seemed that they all shared the same heart. Her staff were also very diverse but the one thing they had in common was their genuine love for people. Analise always knew that she was meant to do that type of work, she couldn't see herself in any other role. She and her staff certainly weren't in the profession for the money, the nonprofit sector was surely a financial challenge at times. Her best friend Diana thought she was silly for not accepting the job offer with FEMA. But Analise didn't care, she was strong willed and based her decisions on what she thought would be for the greater good.

Mija, you cannot save everyone, Nana wrote back in chicken-scratch like penmanship. Analise attempted to get some of her cousins back home to help Nana with emailing instead of handwriting her letters, but she refused. "Typing a letter is the most impersonal thing ever", she said. Nana continued to write an occasional letter to Analise, although the letters were getting more difficult to read with each passing year. Analise accepted the fact that her nana would not live forever, as she would have loved her to.

Analise wrote: *Nana, I had a dream that I was submerged in water and there were people drowning around me, children included. I tried my best to save everyone, but my arms were not enough to save them all. Mija, you cannot save everyone,* she wrote back once again. Analise was hard on herself, she was so passionate about the work that at times it was all consuming, she didn't know how to live a balanced life. She hadn't planned on marrying or having children; it simply wasn't a part of her plan. She loved children but didn't want to bring a child into the world, a world of uncertainty and sometimes unpreventable pain.

She wasn't always conflicted, it was later in her career that her outlook began to change. She was struggling with why these disasters happen, without warning, to some of the most vulnerable of people. She saw the effects of earthquakes, floods, tsunami's and everything in between. Although she was on the front line, in all the turmoil, she maintained her composure, like a true professional. Early on she learned to control her emotions. She thought it was the best decision she could have made because it enabled her to make swift and sound decisions that she was required to do.

Analise was raised in a traditional Catholic home. She didn't label herself a catholic nor had any other religious affiliation. She decided years before that she would not be defined by someone else's beliefs. Her parents were disappointed by her stance, especially because she had attended catholic school growing up. They were devout Catholics, but she just wouldn't accept the religion. She really didn't know what she believed in, besides mankind. She had the conversation with Nana a few times. She listened closely to Nana's views on religion and on life; she was a very unique individual. Analise didn't understand why she did some of the things she did. She thought, *who else has a statue of Buddha, a Menorah, a candle of the Virgen Mary, and a few other religious figures on top of their mantel, in the same house?* Analise didn't quite understand, until she went to visit, the Christmas before Nana passed.

"Mija, I will tell you why I have these religious symbols displayed." Analise looked like a small child again, as she listened to the explanation. Of course, Nana was brilliant in all her ways and she knew that the explanation would be compelling.

"I have purposely placed these figures here so that all of my grandchildren would know that I accept their beliefs, whatever they may be. You see the love that I have for you all is unconditional. I believe that conditions are what people place on others when they disagree with their views. Because my love is unconditional, it means that I welcome your beliefs, and in fact I *want* you to figure out what it is you actually believe, for yourself."

Analise was more impressed with Nana that day, than ever before. In Nana's eyes she could do no wrong, every decision would be accepted because of her unconditional love for her. Analise thought she believed in God, like Jesus Christ, but she felt less and less connected as time went on.

Analise was on her way to India, where there had been a series of flooding near the Southwest Brahmaputra River. Her best friend, Diana offered to take her to the airport, as her visit home to Denver was cut short.

"You know Ana, I tell you this all the time, but I'll tell you again, I am so proud to have someone as amazing as you in my life." Diana was a good friend to Analise and although Diana missed having her friend, she knew that she had to go.

"I am thankful for your loyalty in friendship over the years Diana." "I don't know why I've been chosen to do this work, it's much bigger than myself and it won't stop calling." The two shared a tight embrace before parting ways.

It was nighttime as Analise boarded the long twenty-hour flight. She gazed out the window from the crammed-up window seat she was assigned to. As she gazed out into the night she thought about the conversation she had with Diana. Why did she have such a servant's heart? Did she choose servanthood, or did it choose her? She supposed that mankind had the ability to choose what they would become but she also recognized that some people would never be complete if they weren't doing what they were created to do. *But who really created us anyway,* she thought...*and why?*

She was taught that God created human beings to serve him,

but she wasn't convinced that it was the sole purpose. Why are we even here? Could it be that we simply belong to the universe and not to any one being, like the stars? She had heard of many stories throughout her life of spiritual encounters that people have had. She thought that maybe these people searched deep enough, asked enough questions and had just the right amount of faith, or doubt, to have a spiritual experience. She was bewildered by the notion that some people go through life confused about what they believe, and they do so their entire lives. And then there's the folks who don't believe in anything. Certainly, there is something bigger than us; perhaps it's energy, she thought. And then there's the scientific, mathematical, and historical explanations. Does anybody really know? Can anyone be sure?

As the sun arose, Analise thanked her ancestors for bringing her there safely. She was taught to have a heart of gratitude and she was grateful for even the small things. She saw the beauty in things that a lot of other people overlooked. She had experienced so many things that, she could never describe how they truly affected her. She could not describe what it felt like to see destruction and not being able to work fast enough to help relieve the pain. She couldn't describe the cries of mothers and babies. With all that goes on in the world, she knew that she could not stand by and watch others suffer while she did nothing. As long as she was able, she would continue her work. She wasn't always sure about how she found the strength to continue but something was certainly driving her. *Nana, any good God would not allow his creation to suffer the way I have seen suffering*, she wrote in one of her last letters.

Analise would be working in India for at least the next six months. The community she was working with were mainly Buddhists. Never had Analise seen such a loyalty and commitment to a belief system. She thought that perhaps people needed something bigger than themselves, to believe in, in order to prevent them from feeling completely hopeless. It made sense that if you had an infinite power on your side, that you could overcome anything. Analise witnessed firsthand how the community practiced their beliefs and gained a better understanding of why they believed the way they did. *I suppose people are more alike than they would like to admit,* she wrote in a letter to Nana. Analise received a call from her father, Juanito, one evening, which was early morning for him.

"Hi baby girl, I hate to bother because I know you're busy." "I'm calling to tell you that Nana has been asking for you."

"I spoke to her the other day dad," Analise responded. "And I just sent her a letter last week."

"I know, and she loves receiving your letters, but she is asking for you, more than usual." Analise thought it to be strange but she reassured him that she would call her soon.

"I think you should come to see your nana as soon as your job there is completed." Analise could sense a bit of urgency in her father's voice.

"I will get there as soon as I can dad."

Over the next few weeks, Analise hadn't received a letter back from Nana, which had never happened. She felt that perhaps her dad wasn't telling her everything and that it was a strong possibility that Nana was not doing well. Analise worked day and night to finish up her job so she could get back to the states. When she returned, she immediately headed to see Nana. Analise was tired and jet lagged but felt that she should go anyway. The car ride from the airport to the yellow house on Sherman, never seemed further, she couldn't get there fast enough. The car felt as though it was in slow motion.

As she traveled through the darkness, scenes of Nana's life flashed through her mind. She envisioned the black shoes and apron looking dresses that she would wear. She could see Nana both as a younger woman and as an old fragile woman. She thought about Nana's life. *If today is the day I have to let Nana go, then I guess I will have to assume that she has fulfilled her purpose here,* she reasoned with herself. *And time? What is the purpose of time anyway? And why couldn't it just slow down*, she asked herself. She then realized that it was selfish to want to keep Nana for a while longer; the thought of losing her would surely change her forever. Analise thought about how much she still needed Nana, as if she were still a small child. She knew her Nana still saw her as that small child too.

Analise thought: *If God is merciful, then why would he take someone away, when he knew it would hurt others, she pondered. God is supposed to be all knowing, why than wouldn't he know how losing someone could torment their loved one forever? People say that God is good, but what does that really mean? Does that mean that he is good when everything is going well for them? What about when things are not going so well? That's when people tend to blame God.* With all of the unanswered questions Analise had, she figured that she didn't need the confusion in her life.

And so, with the unwanted confusion, she decided she would not believe in any one God. She did however believe in a source of life; a source of life that looked like a running stream or a well-established tree. Something that consistently grew to give others life, is the only thing she believed in. And the unexplainable occurrences that people experienced, Analise concluded they were a way of keeping people hopeful. A merciful gesture was the universe's way of keeping peoples' hopes and dreams afloat. Who doesn't like to hear about miracles and the unexplainable anyway? But would people rather live a lie or know the truth, she wondered. In Nana's case, Analise didn't really want to know the complete truth.

And even though she had many questions about Nana's life, she thought that she would somehow be ruined, if she knew everything. Perhaps Nana purposely planned it that way all along. She thought about how much Nana wanted to be like a symbolic tree, deeply rooted in love and wisdom. A tree that had many branches that fed off of that main source. She thought about how Nana accepted being that tree that gave life to others, who then gave life to others. Her legacy would be something that would live forever. Everyone should want to be remembered for something great, when their spirits leave their bodies, she thought. Analise somehow knew that some of the things Nana said were a fallacy. Analise would try to piece timelines together and some things simply didn't add up. She hadn't asked Nana about such details, out of respect and because in some strange way, Analise wanted to believe the things she said. Some things were just too special and Analise figured, whether they were true or not, they made a positive impact on her life, and she wouldn't discredit that fact.

"Nana, I'm here," Analise softly said as she opened the screen door. There was no response, so she proceeded to the kitchen which was on the way to the bedroom. She was greeted by her dad who was drinking his coffee at the table. She could tell that he was tired. He looked as though he hadn't slept in days. "Dad, I'm here, what's going on?"

"Your nana is not well Analise."

"I know dad," I could feel it and I tried to get here as soon as I could."

Analise knew that had she arrived sooner, Nana would have been upset with her. Nana believed in her work and once told Analise, "You have been chosen for this work." She somehow made each of her grandchildren feel like they were her favorite but Analise knew deep down that she loved them all equally. Analise also knew that Nana would rather have her out doing work for the greater good, than at home taking care of her; it was her selfless way.

While Analise was in India, she felt that things must have been getting bad if she was asking to see her more than usual. Intuition is something Analise felt very strongly about. And she knew that she was in a predestined moment. What would the last conversation with Nana be like she had wondered. Would she ask Nana if she was proud of her? Would she tell Nana how much she has influenced her life? Would Analise hear something she didn't want to hear?

"Your nana is waiting for you," her dad faintly said.

As Analise began her walk over to her room, she suddenly

became without thoughts or words, which rarely occurred. Her first look at Nana was that of heartache and in that moment, she truly became that small child she once was. Nana was softly sleeping, her long hair sitting past her shoulders, which was a rare sight. She could probably count the few times she saw Nana without a tight bun on the top of her head. Analise gently grabbed her hand as she opened her eyes. She could see the relief in her eyes and Analise was so happy that she had made it in time.

"Analise, my beautiful butterfly."

"I'm here Nana."

"I am so glad to see you," Nana said.

Each spoken word seemed like a challenge, as she was very weak. But somehow, she was more than certain about the content of her words, she possessed full senses and grace, as she always had. "I am weak, but my mind is full of strength and wonder," she told Analise. "I don't know where I'm going mija, but I know that in that place I will continue to be filled with love and joy, as I have my entire life." Analise was attentive, with bright eyes of an enlightened child. "You, my granddaughter need not worry or be saddened by what comes next. You see, I have lived every day of my life, consuming things that I could share. I have lived a life of wonder and magic in my own mind." Analise wasn't sure she wanted the conversation to lead to where she thought it was going. "I have to tell you something, mija."

"Yes Nana," Analise obliged.

"Today I will give you the keys to my world."

Analise then became bewildered.

"You see, the universe had more than one plan for me. I was chosen to be a mother, I was chosen to be a grandmother. And I thanked the universe for the privilege. But, I was also chosen to be other things in life. You see, we are not just meant to be one thing in life. Many paths have been paved and they are all inter twined. You may be on a certain path for a while and then over to another path at another time. Along the overall journey, we encounter those who were meant to be there at that time. Along my journey, I would look back to see my children and grandchildren watching whatever I did. You all caused me to be more than what I should have been. I became a dreamer, a provider, a storyteller. If I could not accomplish everything in life, I wanted you all to believe that you could. So, I had to transform my mind to places and experiences that wouldn't have otherwise happened."

"I don't understand Nana."

"Mija, I am going to leave you for a while, but you must promise me that you will never forget the things that I have taught you."

"Of course, I promise you I won't forget Nana."

"I am so proud of the woman you are, and I want you to know that you are doing things that I wasn't able to do. You have a calling and you are on a very noble path. There aren't very many people who would sacrifice their whole life for the sake of others. You are unselfish and valued more than you'll ever know. Your reward will be that of a beautiful life. A life that people will admire and one that will be an example for others to follow, the universe needs people like you to strengthen the earth. I know that you are struggling with what it is you believe, and I understand it. These are things that you will have to figure out on your own and they will come in due time."

"I know Nana," you have always supported me in everything I do."

"That was my life's purpose." "Had I not shared my *experiences* with you all, you wouldn't see the bountiful possibilities that the world possesses."

At that moment, it was confirmed that some of the stories Nana told her, hadn't actually happened, they were somewhat parables. And Analise understood why she did it. She had always wondered how Nana traveled the world but didn't have any pictures of her actually being in those places. It's as though she had lived numerous other lifetimes. Nana had an answer for everything and said that she didn't take pictures because her memories were embedded in her mind.

"Nana, I know your love for all of us is immeasurable and that you have done the very best you could, I thank you for it all. I just don't want you to leave me; I won't have anyone to look up to anymore."

"Oh, mija, you will always have me to look up to, whether I'm physically here or not. Death is the natural progression of life, we were born to die. It is now your turn to be the person, that others look up to, especially your children and your grandchildren. The difference between you and I is the fact that you are actually experiencing a lifetime of seeing the world in the flesh."

Analise never felt so proud of who she had become until that moment. No other words of pride would ever compare to the sentiment of her nana.

"Now, go to my jewelry box and open the bottom drawer."

"Nana, I don't want any of your jewelry."

Nana chuckled ever so girlishly at what she said. Analise obediently got up and walked over to the jewelry box. As she opened up the bottom drawer, she saw nothing but pearls and vintage pins. Nana said, "Keep looking." Analise found a key buried under the pieces of jewelry.

"This Nana?"

And as Analise held up an old, rusty key, she said, "That's it." I'm not going to tell you what the key opens right now but you will find its proper place, when it's time." Every recollection Analise had of Nana were of mystery and enchantment and this time was no different.

"Okay Nana, I will put this key in a safe place for another time." Nana nodded her head; she was getting tired. "Rest Nana, I will stay here with you until you are ready." Nana then slowly closed her eyes.

Analise slept alongside Nana that evening; she held her with all the love she had in her heart. Analise had never loved harder than she did that night. She had known love, love for the people of the world, love for the lost, love for the lonely, love for the helpless. The love that radiated from her soul that evening was unlike anything she had ever given. She prayed to the universe, asking that they could be frozen in time. She just didn't know how she could let go and wanted to stop the inevitable; everything was all too real. As days went on Nana had many visitors. At times, Analise thought that it was too much for her, but Nana never turned anyone away. She overheard some of the conversations and some of the conversations Nana requested be private; everyone respected her wishes. It was as though she held on until she saw every last family member.

After Nana Ofelia passed, Analise stood in town for a while. It was wintertime in Denver, and the snow began to fall. As Analise left her father's house one night, she slipped on some ice. As she struggled to get up, she wondered how she had fallen since she was being extra careful in avoiding the patches of ice. She attempted to get up a few times but was unable to stand, her ankles were in excruciating pain. And just as she made another attempt, she fell back again. With tears running down her face, she saw a shadow on her right side. She looked again and saw an elderly woman standing over her. Analise was a bit frightened but desperate for help.

"Are you ok dear?" the woman asked.

"Can you hand me my phone Ma'am," Analise asked her.

The woman wasn't anyone Analise knew, and she knew of most of the neighbors on the block. What was this older lady doing out in such bad weather, late at night, Analise wondered. The woman extended out her hand to help Analise up, but she declined the offer, as she didn't want the woman to get injured.

"Please just hand me my phone."

The woman insisted by saying, "Dear, you shouldn't doubt other people's strengths."

Just as the woman said that, Analise felt like she knew the woman, there was something familiar about her. Perhaps it was her eyes or her voice; she found it strange. As the woman's arm remained extended, Analise finally grabbed her hand. The woman was stronger than she expected. With the woman's help, Analise was able to make it to her parent's steps. The lady handed her the phone and Analise started to dial her dad's number. She looked over to thank the lady but there was no one there; she wondered where the lady had gone. There were no tracks anywhere and no sight of anyone. Analise's dad came out and helped her into the house; she didn't tell him about the strange encounter.

That night, after she returned from the hospital, she couldn't sleep thinking about the encounter. As Analise awoke the following morning, she saw a beautiful sunrise peeping through the bay window. After some thought about the encounter, she figured out exactly why it must have happened. She knew Nana would always be with her and would manifest her love for her as long as she lived. She smiled as she concluded that Nana must have sent the woman to help her, as Analise was someone who lived her life helping others. She accepted it as a small token of gratitude from Nana.

She also concluded that, Nana was reminding her to never change, never stop helping people and she will always be helped in her own time of need. Analise thought it was such a beautiful message and she would never forget it. Over the years, she would be shopping in a store, when someone would unexpectedly appear to help her, without her asking. These individuals held full blown conversations with her, basically concerned with her well-being. It became a common occurrence; it seemed like Nana had her own way of showing Analise that she was always with her. Analise never shared the occurrences with anyone, she just knew what it was.

After a few years, Analise eventually got married to a wonderful man and they had a couple of children, a boy and a girl. She continued her work, as an independent consultant for disaster relief organizations. She wanted to stay at home to raise her children, she was a very good mother. She thanked the universe for her children daily and felt very blessed to be entrusted to raise children of her own. She no longer struggled with what she believed in because of where life had brought her. She still wasn't religious, nor would she persuade her children to believe in anything besides, the human heart, the giving soul, the kind spirit. And the universe. A universe that will conspire the good for you, when you learn to give love freely. She knew her children would be blessed because she would teach them everything that Nana taught her.

Analise began to feel that she wanted to do something different in her humanitarian work. Her friends, a couple, Jose and Elena who were from the United States, had been pastoring a church in Honduras for a few years. They invited Analise to visit their village to see if she would be willing to do some work there. After some time, she decided that she would go. As she traveled deep into the mountains, she thought the landscape was beautiful; it reminded her of Colorado, but much greener. She immediately felt like she was strangely connected to the country, although she had never been there before. She spoke decent Spanish and wanted to learn more. She was certain that by spending time there, she would become a better speaker. The pastors of the church set up activities throughout the couple of weeks that she would be visiting. There were a few missionaries visiting at the same time, it was orchestrated that way. Some of the missionaries had been there a few times and the pastors thought it would be a good idea for Analise to see the work that they were doing. She met the missionaries, who were all so different. They varied in age and backgrounds, but Analise could tell that they shared the same heart. She recognized the heartbeat of the missionaries, as she too had a heart to serve. She had done some missionary work earlier on in her career, caring for orphans, until she was offered administrative roles. It had been a long time, and somehow this time everything felt different to her.

The group of missionaries had established a good rapport with the community and the people welcomed them with arms wide open. The group, including Analise, began the first few days by working in the village school. Analise met the school children and hadn't realized until then, just how fortunate her own children were. She and her husband were able to financially provide for them with ease. She thought about why certain people are born into certain situations. She felt saddened by the living conditions of the people of the village, their makeshift homes had no electricity or running water. And even though the children lacked basic human needs, they were still able to smile.

Analise felt emotional about the things she witnessed throughout the weeks. It was as if she was looking through a different set of eyes. It almost felt like she was awakened, her eyes were being unveiled, her heart was being revived. She didn't understand what was happening to her, but she welcomed it nonetheless. She met many people during her trip to Honduras. She met single mothers who were struggling to feed their children. She met children with special needs, who she knew lacked resources that they needed, in the village. She met the orphaned children who she felt empathy for. She met a twelve-year old boy named Christian, who she fell in love with. She thought about how, if she could, she would be able to give him a better life. Her heart broke for him and the other vulnerable children.

One day the team took a catered meal to some students at the school. The children were overtaken with joy; their eyes lit up like fireworks on the Fourth of July. She became confused when she witnessed the children packing up their food after just taking a few bites. The teachers explained that the children wanted to take their meals home to share with their families. She thought about what the world would look like if everyone was more like those children. During the days she spent in the village, she was being transformed.

The last day she was there, the team went to visit the pastors church, that was set high on a hill. She chose to sit near the window, as it was a very warm evening. The shutters were open, and she could see the mountainous landscape in the background. As the service was about to begin, she saw five little girls, dressed in beautiful long dresses, each adorned in vivid color. As she stared at the girls, she thought, that is what angels must look like. As the service began, the girls lined up in the front of the church. The music began to play, and the girls danced their tiny hearts out, with the same amount of enthusiasm to each song. Their movements were in sync and they took much pride in playing such a vital role in the church.

As Analise watched the angels dance, she was moved and began to weep. She could see pure light in the faces of the young girls. She remembered one of the girls from earlier in the week; her name was Alice. Analise learned that she had severe learning disabilities. Her mother explained that Alice's father didn't want her to attend school because he thought she couldn't learn anyway; Analise saw the opposite that evening. She knew that Alice could learn, she knew that Alice could soar with wings like eagles. As tears ran down Analise's face, she peered out the window, in awe of the beautiful landscape.

In that exact moment, at forty years of age, she encountered a real experience with God. She had never felt him before, she knew it was him, she could not deny it. She immediately felt remorse, for questioning her beliefs in the previous years. That night she fully surrendered herself to God. She was amazed that God led her deep into the mountains, in Honduras, to show her how real he is. She believed that he must have been there all her years, but she wasn't ready to hear his voice. She recalled seeing God through the faces of the children she had met throughout the week. She saw God in a lot of instances during her time there. She knew she would never be the same again.

As she wiped her tears, thinking about what would come next for her, she heard a whisper. She felt Nana Ofelia whispering how proud she was of her. Analise was reassured that she was exactly where she was supposed to be. After getting to know the other missionaries, she realized more than ever, that she was one of them. They had the same heart, a heart to serve. She vowed to be open to where God would lead her next. A year later, she and her family moved to Honduras where she continued her work as a missionary. Analise finally felt like many of life's questions that she had, had been revealed. Everything but one thing...the key Nana gave her. She hadn't gone searching for answers because she needed to figure out what she believed in first and she had been on a spiritual journey for five years. Her children were growing more curious about life and she knew that she couldn't possibly have all the right answers; she felt she needed reinforcement and Nana wasn't there to turn to. Therefore, the search to find what the key unlocked began.

Analise asked her father about the key but he had no idea what it opened. Analise went to the next person who might have been able to help, her cousin Julian. Since Julian had inherited the house and everything in it, he must have known something, she hoped.

"Julian, Nana gave me this key, do you know what it opens?"

"I have no idea Analise," he said.

"There must be some clue to help us find what it unlocks."

"I cleaned out most of everything in the house," he responded.

They both sat in the living room, in the yellow house, on Sherman, bewildered by the significance of the key. They looked at each other like they knew what the other was thinking. Surely Nana had a purpose for leaving the key, she was far too brilliant and too intentional. Her intentional nature was evidenced by her book of recipes showing up to their cousin Clarissa, a year after her death. Everything with Nana had seemed so well thought out. She was still impacting people, even though she was no longer there. The two of them searched the house, day in and day out looking for clues. Since the house had been remodeled, everything inside was fairly new. Initially they had no luck in finding any clues and so Analise became obsessed with the possibilities, as she believed that the quest was happening at the right time. As she and Julian sat in the kitchen one afternoon, they heard the old coo coo clock going off. They both looked at each other in sequence. The only thing that remained untouched in the house was the old, annoying, coo coo clock that still hung in what used to be Nana's bedroom. Nana claimed she got the clock on a trip that she took to Germany. They ran, like kids to the room and immediately took the clock down. In the back of the clock, just as they suspected was a folded-up note that read:

Analise, I really didn't get this clock from Germany, I actually got it from the thrift store on Broadway. But I did go to Germany, I went to Germany and I've been around the world. Go to this address, where you'll learn of my adventures and bear witness to my travels with your own eyes.

Analise and Julian jumped in the car and headed west toward the mountains. The address was barely legible, but they made out the numbers 111 Saddle Road. The map on Analise's phone led them to Bear Creek, Colorado, a secluded town about an hour outside of Denver. The two of them were excited to see what lie ahead of them. The town seemed uninhabited with the exception of a few elk and deer. As they finally found what they thought must have been the address, they pulled up to undeveloped land.

"What are we doing here?" Julian asked Analise.

"I don't understand," she responded.

Analise got out of the car and looked around. She saw nothing that she would need a key for. It was getting dark and she knew time was running out. She looked around again and could finally see some sort of structure in the distance. She took off running as fast as she could, Julian trying to catch up.

"Wait Analise!"

The structure turned out to be a small shack. She quickly turned the key and opened the old door as it creaked very loudly, they went in. Analise was astonished by what she saw. Books, books, lots of them! She was confused and curious at the same time, so she started taking a closer look. It was definitely a library. A dusty library but a very well-organized library, nonetheless. She grabbed a random book off the shelf; it was a travel book of Greece. Inside the book were notes, certain things highlighted, and other pages of stories written, hidden within. As they continued to explore, they discovered that each booked contained intricate thoughts and ideas. Some books had a specific note to someone in the family, that stated things like, *Analise, go there, it's beautiful.* The collection included several travel books but also included books of poetry, philosophy, math, religion, art and other random topics.

She and Julian finally began to figure out why Nana was such a brilliant mind, with knowledge of things they couldn't comprehend. On another shelf she found a section of journals in chronological order that were handwritten by Nana. The journals were dated as recent as up to the last year she was alive. In the contents of the journals, Analise would learn everything she ever needed to know about Nana; the dreamer, the believer, the storyteller, the wise-woman. Analise was so grateful that Nana deemed her worthy to share her true self with her. She sat and wept as she thought about why Nana felt the need to do all of it. Why had she created something so magical, she wondered? Analise decided to bring the small shack to life. She wanted to share everything with the family, so she decided to create a space where they could retreat to. A quiet place filled with every dream that Nana had for the entire family.

Analise got inspired to write her own journals for her children that could be shared for generations to come. It seems as though Nana started a trend of storytelling. Analise was honored to be the granddaughter of someone who lived a wonderous life. Nana was an integral piece to Analise's future and she believed that Nana Ofelia was the most magnificent woman she had ever known.

CHAPTER SEVEN

The Fearless Explorer

.

Today I will write about the most magnificent woman I know.
This woman is pure light, a shining star, a dreamer, a free bird.
Inscribing a description to paper has been a difficult thing to do,
as even the most sophisticated wording and elegant writing could
not do justice, in describing such a brilliant human being.

ANALISE WAS WRITING A BOOK, A COLLECTION OF SHORT STORIES, AS
TOLD BY VARIOUS FAMILY MEMBERS, ABOUT NANA OFELIA'S LIFE. She
also referred to the many journals and notes that Nana left the family,
to help complete the book.

Ofelia Rosas was born on January 1, 1919. She was destined
for greatness, even during an era when women were less encouraged
to pursue their personal dreams. Even without encouragement she
creatively found a way to live her dreams. *Dreams are seeds planted*
in our hearts, Nana wrote in one of her many journals. She believed
that there was more than one way to fulfill a dream. *Some dreams*
will be realized through other people and some dreams are experienced
through transcending our inner thoughts, she wrote. She lived a lifetime
of fulfilling her realization of the seeds that had been planted in her

heart. She was determined to live the kind of life that she could be proud enough of to share with her family, a life that was filled with incomparable experiences. The experiences and wisdom she would share were unconventional indeed.

Ofelia Rosas was a very curious young girl who asked a ton of questions, so many questions in fact, that it resulted into occasional trouble. At times people found her curiosity to be a bit disruptive. She always had a follow-up question to the previous question; and some people didn't have the patience to deal with her. It was either a lack of patience on their part, or perhaps she was just brighter than most, and it caused them to grow frustrated with her persistence of increased knowledge. She was bright, there was no doubt about it. She had a deeper understanding that there was an entire world out beyond the corn fields that she was surrounded by and she was determined to find a way to explore it. Text books were at times hard to come by, in the small towns where Ofelia and her family lived. Her school attendance was not consistent, but she did love to learn. Growing up in a family of ten kids, certainly had its challenges, nonetheless, she made sure to establish her place in the family.

Ofelia was the youngest and she was constantly learning from her older siblings. Her parents immigrated from Mexico to California to work in the fields where they picked various fruits and vegetables. The Rosas family traveled from town to town, wherever work was available. Ofelia's parents didn't have expectations for their children, other than them growing up to be honest, hardworking people. It seemed natural that their children would also make a living working in the fields while raising families of their own. When Ofelia got settled into a new school in a new town, the family would be uprooted again. Ofelia would work in the fields before and after school every day. If there was a lot of work to be done, she and her siblings weren't allowed to go to school at all. She definitely dreaded those days, they seemed to be the longest days of her life.

One particular year, the Rosas family was expected to stay

working in the fields of the Silicon Valley for that entire year. Ofelia had never been so excited; she was ten years old. She would follow a few of her siblings to school, one behind the other, like a tiny army of their own. The older, more physically capable siblings were no longer allowed to go to school, just the younger children. Since most of the schools were in small towns, it wasn't uncommon that various aged children be grouped into a single classroom. Ofelia was usually placed with a few of her older siblings and with other children up to fourteen years old. She was fascinated by classrooms; everything from the chalk boards to the maps hanging on the walls excited her. It was an escape from the reality of the long hours that she spent in the fields. Attending school made her feel like she could, if even temporarily, be someone else. She admired teachers and emulated them during her free time in the fields.

Although Ofelia was growing up in less than desirable conditions, she was a joyful child. She enjoyed spending time playing with her siblings, but she also equally enjoyed her time alone. She was an imaginative child, she created imaginary friends, as though interaction with her numerous siblings wasn't sufficient. She later realized that she must've created imaginary friends out of her need to interact with a variety of people. Every friend was in fact very different. She imagined male and female friends of different races. Some of them were much older than herself, adult-like. The conversations she had with her friends had a lot of depth. She shared her darkest secrets and most inner thoughts with them. She also shared the visions that she had for her life; her friends were always a positive influence. Her family hadn't always accepted her imaginary friends; they all agreed that Ofelia was quite unique.

Her sister Lourdes accepted her the way she was, although she didn't fully comprehend how her complex mind worked. Nonetheless, her love for her was greater than her understanding. Ofelia wasn't well accepted by children at school either. Her classmates thought she was strange and perhaps a little slow. She admitted that she was a little slow, not in thought process but rather in formal learning. She grasped concepts but struggled with processes.

She often wondered about other places; she had only been to California and Mexico at that point. The family would take a one-week vacation to Mexico during the summer to visit extended family. Since she recognized that life was so different in Mexico, she concluded that there must be even more out in the world. She envisioned different landscapes and even more unique people, like herself. She vowed to experience everything she could, when she was old enough to do so. As she worked in the fields, she talked to the birds. "Where do your travels lead you to today blessed ones?" she asked them as they landed near her. She thought that if she could be any animal, it would be a bird. If she were a bird, she would have complete freedom to take to the skies and see everything that was out in the world; her possibilities would certainly be endless. At times her curiosity was her worst enemy. Since expectations of her life were rarely, if ever, communicated by her parents, she knew she would have to establish expectations for her own life; she learned that at a very young age.

"Lourdes, wait for me!" Ofelia yelled out to her older sister as they ran to the school house. Lourdes was just two years older, they were different yet very close. Lourdes did her best to look after her, especially when the students in class were cruel to her.

"Hurry up Paloma!" (Paloma is a Spanish word, translated to white dove) She nicknamed Ofelia Paloma due to her infatuation with birds.

"I'm running as fast as I can, your legs are longer than mine!"

Ofelia was a petit child, who looked even younger than she was. Lourdes waited for her tiny sister and quickly grabbed her by the hand, as they ran through the corn fields. "We are going to be late Lourdes!" "You know I hate being late for school," she uttered as she tried to regain breath to her lungs.

"No, we're not! And so, what if we're late anyway, school is pointless! People like us don't need school Paloma."

Lourdes wasn't nearly as excited as Ofelia and didn't see the value in school. She had difficulty getting along with the other kids, so much in fact that she would be sent home for fighting with them. She would rather work in the fields instead of going to school anyway. She and Ofelia's personality couldn't be any different.

"But I love school!" tiny Ofelia yelled out with her last breath as they arrived at the school house.

"Whatever you say," Lourdes nonchalantly said.

As they entered the classroom, Ofelia enthusiastically sat in the front row, eager to learn by asking the teacher a million questions. "Now class, remember, we only speak English in this classroom," the teacher said as she pointed to the sign near the door that read *English Only*. None of the students objected. The students began their day by residing the Pledge of Allegiance; Ofelia didn't understand the significance of the pledge but nonetheless emulated the teacher, who seemed to boast with pride as she led the class. Tiny Ofelia stood as tall as she could, in her homemade lavender colored dress that her mother made for her, with her chin lifted high.

The teacher was a white woman, *La Gringa*, as the Mexican students called her. She was stern but overall compassionate towards the students. Most of the students were immigrant children who spoke very little English, if any at all. The school severely lacked resources because it was in a rural county, but the teachers maximized what little they had. That particular teacher refused to swat the students for speaking Spanish, like some of the other teachers had chosen to do. Years later, Ofelia concluded that the teacher must have been a decent woman, as she accepted that it wasn't the kids' fault that Spanish was their first language. Ofelia and her siblings spoke English fluently; they learned a lot of new words from speaking to the farmers they worked for. Language wasn't necessarily a barrier for them.

Spanish was spoken by their parents in the home; their parents were less interested in learning to speak English. Ofelia was different and more determined than anyone in her family to learn proper English, and anything else she could for that matter. It seemed that her sponge like mind was bigger than her tiny body. Day after day, Ofelia sat in the front of the classroom soaking up the teachers every word. The teacher read excerpts from Romeo and Juliet and asked the students for their interpretation of the story to see if they were being attentive. Ofelia immediately raised her hand, "They died for love," she said. The teacher was well aware that Ofelia was extremely attentive. She asked her to read the last sentence from the story, but Ofelia declined her offer. The teacher then offered to help her read it; she again refused. The teacher went over and kneeled beside her chair, she whispered, "I know that you don't know how to read but I will help you." Ofelia wasn't ready and felt that she would be embarrassed in front of her peers.

That day, ten-year old Ofelia became infuriated that she was unable to read, and she decided that she would learn to read no matter what she had to do. She went to school early and left late, whenever she could, to get extra help from the teacher. "Ofelia, please tell your parents that I would love for them to attend Family Night next week." Her parents rarely attended school functions due to the language barrier. They mainly relied on their children for translation, if they absolutely had to speak to a teacher. To Ofelia's surprise, her parents attended Family Night that particular evening.

"I believe Ofelia has a learning disability," the teacher told an older sibling, who was translating.

Ofelia's parents didn't fully understand what having a learning disability meant. The teacher proceeded to explain, "Ofelia sees words and letters backwards." With great regret on her face, she reluctantly said, "We do not have the resources at this school to help your daughter." She regained her composure and proceeded, "The nearest school that can help with this kind of issue is about fifty miles away." "If you don't get her the help she needs, I don't believe that she will ever be able to read." Her parents didn't seem very concerned by what she said. They lacked understanding about the impact that having a learning disability would have on Ofelia's future. They ultimately knew that they would not be able to uproot the family fifty miles away, to a town with no work, to get Ofelia, help with her learning disability. It was simply not an option.

Ofelia was saddened after she overheard what the teacher said. The horrifying thought that she may never read, is something she refused to accept. How could she possibly learn if she couldn't read she wondered? She was well aware that most knowledge she would ever need, would come straight out of books. She knew something must have been wrong because letters were a blur when she looked at books.

After the informal diagnosis, Ofelia became disengaged at school. At times she didn't want to go, which was extremely out of character. She felt disappointed in herself for not learning to read and she was giving up. She knew she would never get the help she needed, and she did not expect for her family to be uprooted for her sake. The school year came to an end, and without much progress, Ofelia began her summer working in the unbearable California heat. Some days she thought she was losing her mind as her tiny body and her mind felt disconnected. At times her tiny hands worked until they became hard and bled. Her family surely wasn't very sympathetic, as their hands mirrored hers.

As the birds came to pay Ofelia a visit, she could hear one of them silently whispering to her. "You can learn anything you want to learn," the black bird softly said. Ofelia fell to her knees as she wept in defeat; she didn't believe the bird that day. Every day after that for the entire summer, the same bird arrived with the same message of hope. She knew it was the same bird because the bird seemed to have difficulty flying. The bird had a slow start as it took to the sky but once it gained momentum it graciously fell in line with the others. After some time, it dawned on her, that perhaps the bird was right, perhaps it knew more than what she gave it credit for. She thought about how many miracles the bird might have seen in its lifetime. The bird itself was a miracle, she thought. If the bird found a way to fly, how much more could she find a way to do the same? She finally began to believe that she could accomplish anything and for the next few years, she would not be seen without a book in hand. The teachers at her school were in disbelief, that someone with such a severe learning disability, could overcome such a challenge. Not only did Ofelia overcome but she was thriving, soon she became advanced and was one of the brightest students in the school.

Her family continued living in the small rural county for the next five years. Work was plentiful, and they had no reason to move, which satisfied her greatly. She had finally made a few friends at school and was content with how life was going during that time. However, she felt that life had bigger plans for her and she couldn't wait to see what she would become. She spent the next couple of years devising a plan.

"Lourdes, can you believe we are in our final years of school, time is moving so fast," Ofelia said. "What do you want to do after school?" Ofelia asked her sister.

"What do you mean Paloma? I'm going to stay here and help Mami and Papi take care of the house."

By that time, some of the older siblings had gone on to establish families of their own. Some of them stayed, and some of them moved away different towns.

"Not me, Lourdes, I need to fly away!"

Lourdes knew that being in the small town would not be enough to satisfy her sister's curiosity forever. Ofelia needed to experience the world, or her spirit would surely die, the both of them fully understood that. Lourdes accepted her sister's curiosity although she undoubtedly knew that when Ofelia left her, a part of herself would die.

Ofelia was so mature and yet so childlike with her interactions with Lourdes. Lourdes found some of Ofelia's ideas to be so farfetched, almost to the point that she was entertained. Lourdes doubted that some of her sister's goals would ever be attainable, but she loved her enough to support her in whatever she dreamt possible.

"Lourdes, can you meet me at the pond behind the school-house, tomorrow morning at sunrise?"

"Here we go again with your crazy ideas, Paloma."

"Really, I mean it, you have to come to the pond at sunrise."

"Sister, okay, yes, I'll come," she said as she reluctantly rolled her eyes.

Lourdes was the most loyal person that Ofelia had known up until that point. People rarely told Ofelia no, because she would give a hundred reasons to justify her request. It was much easier for people to oblige, rather than to give a hundred reasons why saying no was a better idea and Lourdes had learned that early on.

"Thank you, sister, for being a perfect sister and thank you for believing in me."

Lourdes smiled as she jokingly said, "I *am* a perfect sister, maybe someday you'll be just like me," as she brushed her shoulder off. Ofelia laughed, and Lourdes grabbed Ofelia's tightly bund hair and pulled it a few inches down, which was one of her pet peeves. But that day Ofelia just laughed at the annoying, loving gesture.

The next morning, before the roosters began to crow, Ofelia jumped out of bed. She quickly began to disassemble the curlers made of torn rags, from her hair. She had anticipated a glorious day! As she sat in front of her vanity mirror, she saw something different, she suddenly viewed herself as a young woman. Even though she was only seventeen years old, she felt a lot more mature that morning. Her hair was flowing, and she remembered her mother's hair, that looked the exact same way. She thought about how the events of the day would break her mother's heart. But she somehow knew that her mother, a woman of very few words, would admire her courage to forge her own path.

Ofelia began to wrap her hair into a tight bun and with every bobby pin she placed around her hair, she recollected her childhood. She recalled the countless conversations with her imaginary friends, the moment she realized that she could read, and the times her older sister protected her. As tears slowly fell from her tender eyes, she refused to allow the tears to be that of sadness. Instead she converted them into tears of happiness, special moments that she would hold near to her heart until the day she died. She felt blessed to have had great childhood memories surrounded by a big family. She loved all of them and would greatly miss each of them. She wasn't sure what the future held but she was certain about the foundation that had been set, by the examples of people she grew up around.

As the sun began to rise, Ofelia could see Lourdes running through the sunflowers. It was a brisk morning and the sunrise was deep purple lined with bright orange, unlike any sunrise she had ever seen. Ofelia sat near the pond next to the old oak tree that hosted her and Lourdes' names. They had carved their names under two stick figures holding hands that resembled two little girls, many years before. "I'm coming Paloma!" her sister yelled. If she knew what was about to transpire, Ofelia was certain that Lourdes wouldn't have been running with such enthusiasm. Lourdes became accustomed to Ofelia's surprises, as she often surprised her with small gifts or nice picnics near the pond.

As Lourdes reached the pond, she could see that there was no picnic nor any tangible gift in sight. "What's going on Paloma?" she asked. Lourdes looked a little closer, as the purple and orange sky intensified. She could see a large green, soldier looking bag laying beneath the oak tree.

"Good morning my beautiful sister," Ofelia said.

"Good morning Paloma, what are you up to now?" she asked.

"I asked you to come here to say good bye Lourdes."

"What do you mean?" Lourdes aversely asked. Although she wasn't sure that she wanted to hear her sister's response.

"I am beginning my journey today!"

"What kind of journey are you talking about?"

"My life journey," she excitedly answered.

Lourdes was confused by what her little sister was actually saying. But if anyone truly knew Ofelia, it was Lourdes. She believed that Ofelia was limitless if presented with the right opportunity; and that frightened Lourdes at times. Up until that point, there was no real opportunity presented that would push Ofelia to something life altering.

"I will be beginning my life journey today Lourdes, look at how the sky is speaking this glorious morning." She sternly proceeded, "It is time, when the universe speaks, we must act."

Lourdes was more practical than her sister and she didn't always buy into Ofelia's jibber about how the universe speaks or how she receives messages through signs and animals. Perhaps Lourdes loved Ofelia so much that she didn't want to crush her spirit, so she had always played along.

And on that particular morning, Lourdes knew that she would have to play along more than she had ever before. "I wanted to personally say good bye my lovely sister." "I didn't have to say good bye, but I do not know when I will see you again." Before Lourdes could say anything, Ofelia wept, happy tears and hugged her sister like never before.

Lourdes slightly pulled away and asked, "Where are you going Paloma?"

"I don't know where I'm going or where I'll end up, all I know is that I must go. Life is calling me, and my soul will never be satisfied until I figure out exactly what I am being called to. Everyone has a destiny sister and now it's my turn to find mine."

"As much as I do not want to see you leave, I know that you will go regardless."

"I have to Lourdes," Ofelia said with a sense of urgency in her voice. "I have waited seventeen years for this very day, and if I wait any longer, I may miss something very important, a clue, a path or a person, I was destined to meet, therefore I must go."

As the two young women stood in silence for a few seconds, they could hear the roar of a train passing through the valley. Lourdes instinctively knew that Ofelia would be on the next train, setting out on her grand adventure. The trains passed through the valley every couple of hours and they weren't passenger trains, they were freight trains that transported supplies, like coal and grain.

Ofelia inevitably knew that the day would come, therefore thoughtfully planned her exit. "Mami and Papi will realize that I'm gone by dinner time, assure them that I am going to be fine and that I will write them as soon as I can." Lourdes was saddened by all that Ofelia said, as it sounded so final. She herself wasn't sure if she would ever see her sister again. "I will come back to visit as soon as I can, I will see you again sister, I promise." There was something convincing about Ofelia's words that could make anyone trust her. And so, Lourdes trusted that it would not be the last time she would see her sister's bright eyes. The two held one another tightly as if they were holding on to mere life, until Ofelia gently let go. She then headed over to the tree, grabbed her bag and began to walk towards the rail road tracks. She didn't want to look back at her sister's sad eyes, so she sped up to avoid further eye contact.

As Lourdes watched her baby sister walk beyond the sunflowers, she knew that she had to let her go. As much as her mind told her to grab Ofelia and shake her out of it, her heart whispered, *Let her fly*. As Ofelia's silhouette began to fade, Lourdes ran her hand over the carved image of the two girls on the oak tree. She knew that when Ofelia returned she would be a full-grown woman. She would return as a woman with life experience, and the thought of seeing happiness on her sister's face, brought her comfort.

Lourdes walked home without her little sister that morning, the sister she had lived to protect. She offered up a prayer to the same universe that Ofelia believed in, with the hope that the universe would protect her, just as she had. As Ofelia ran to the railroad tracks she nearly missed the six o'clock train, that she planned on catching. She had one hundred dollars sewn into a secret pocket inside her homemade skirt, for safe keeping. Ofelia ran as fast as she could, never looking back to the only home she had ever known. She believed that what awaited, would be greater than anything she could experience within the confines of the tiny town she once called home.

And so, Ofelia hooked her left arm onto the handle of the last freight car. She could barely lift her bag up along with her weight; it was more difficult than she anticipated. After she jumped into the car filled with hay, she realized that the journey she was about to embark on would be a challenge. But the challenge didn't stop her, she had her overly determined mind made up. The train traveled for hours further northward. It was getting dark, the fog was thick, and she was cold. She had certainly underestimated the weather conditions and meanwhile wasn't sure where the final destination would find her. She knew that the first night would be the coldest and loneliest. She talked to herself, convincing herself that every night afterward would become easier. *Surely, no good thing comes without sacrifice,* she thought.

She had finally fallen asleep, using her green bag as a pillow. The hay was poking her and so she had to lie as still as she could. That night she had a series of bad dreams. She dreamt of images chasing her, while trying everything they could to prevent her from grasping on to good things. She reached out to touch the ocean water, but the images pulled her back. She ran towards a bright light ahead of her, where she could see a beautiful gold locket illuminated and again she was pulled back. She tried to fight her way through, but the images were stronger than she was. She woke up feeling defeated and doubting herself. Maybe she was searching for something that really didn't exist, she thought.

As the train came to a stop, she knew that it was too late to turn back. In that moment she accepted whatever life would bring, good or bad. As the train stopped she could hear the conductor yelling at another man in the stockyard. Soon a bunch of men came out to help unload the box cars. "I have to get out of here," she said to herself. She veered out to see where the men were gathering. She knew she had to go the opposite direction. As she looked down, she wondered how she had even gotten into the car. The way down seemed much higher than she remembered, she had to move quickly. So, she frantically grabbed her bag and threw it out of the car. She could hear the men's voices getting closer, and with every ounce of strength she had, she grabbed onto the side handle and jumped out of the car; she was covered in hay. She quickly picked up her bag from the ground and threw it over her shoulder and ran from the train as fast as she could.

She didn't know where she was yet; but could see a blue pickup truck speeding down a dirt road. *That's where the town must be,* she thought and so she decided to head in the same direction as the pickup truck. Ofelia passed a few houses while on her way down the road. At one of the houses she saw a couple of children sitting on a swing, on a beautiful wrap around porch. They were drinking lemonade, that Ofelia so desperately wished she could have a drink of. The children didn't seem to notice her, which she found strange because there wasn't anyone else wandering aimlessly on the road, like she was. Clearly, she was not from there. Ofelia was also used to being greeted by everyone she came into contact with, as small towns tend to be more personal. Everyone knew everyone, in the small town she was from. And the people were always very friendly. Ofelia shrugged her shoulders at the lack of interaction as she kept on walking down the road into the unknown. Soon she was heading toward a more well-maintained road, where she could see a few stores and a library. She was starving and already missing her mother's delicious, homemade breakfast. She thought that she should eat, as she would need energy to get through her first day of her life journey.

"May I have some eggs and bacon?" she asked the less than friendly waitress at the restaurant.

"Sure," the waitress slowly answered, as though she was being inconvenienced.

As Ofelia sat at the table near the large window, she could see people walking around the town. It was a Saturday morning, she assumed it was a little busier than usual. While she patiently waited for her food, she took out a book to read to help pass the time. It turns out that books took up the majority of her army looking bag, that's why it was so heavy. She left home with the things that were important to her, and books were her prized possession. Books helped her escape from reality at times and she knew that in this journey she was going to need books to get her through the lonely times that she would encounter. She also brought along the journals she had written. She hoped that someday someone would read her journals and they could learn more about the person she was.

Her food finally arrived at the table after a long wait, and Ofelia scarfed the food down quickly, almost unlady-like. She could see a few of the customers at other tables glaring at her. They must've known she wasn't from the town, she thought. The townspeople were not very friendly at all. She supposed that this was an important part of her journey. *Not everyone is the same and there are no two places alike*, she jotted down in her journal as she took her last bite of her breakfast. Just as she closed her journal, the waitress came over to give her the bill.

The waitress sarcastically said, "You look lost young lady."

Ofelia got offended by her assumption and responded, "No ma'am, I'm not lost, just passing through."

Ofelia knew at that moment that the visit to this town would be short lived. She didn't feel very welcomed since everyone she come into contact with thus far hadn't at least acknowledged her existence; never had she felt so invisible. She decided then that she could never live in a place surrounded by such unfriendly people.

Ofelia was not ignorant to that fact that the world could be cruel, but she had never quite experienced it herself. She knew she could never plant her roots in a place like that, it wasn't pleasurable, at all.

After breakfast, Ofelia wandered around the town, invisible to most; she was people watching. She wanted to go to the library but since it was closed until Monday, she decided she would at least stay in town until then. She went back to the stockyard that night where the train sat stationary. She slept on the hay under the dark night. She slept there for the next couple of nights and just as she expected, her loneliness seemed to subside with each passing night. The first thing Monday morning, Ofelia walked over to the library where she came into contact with the librarian. To her surprise, the librarian was young, like herself. She wore red cat eye glasses and the brightest matted red lipstick that Ofelia had ever seen. She was unlike any librarian that Ofelia had seen before. She was friendly and nothing like the other townspeople that Ofelia had encountered during her short visit.

"May I help you?" the librarian asked.

"Good morning, I'm passing through town and I stayed in town for a couple of days, to visit this library."

"I see, I'm honored that you have stayed around just to visit my library," the librarian kindly responded.

Ofelia could immediately see that the lady took much pride in the library.

"Are you looking for anything in particular?"

"I don't know what I'm looking for, I guess I'll know when I find it," Ofelia responded. The librarian found her vague response peculiar, but she decided to help her look for a good read anyway.

"Well, as you can see there are many interesting books here," the librarian said as she ran her hands across the shelves as if to show off her most treasured possessions. "They are organized very specifically." Ofelia could clearly see that. The librarian could sense that Ofelia wanted to browse by herself. "Feel free to look around and if you have questions, don't hesitate to ask and I'll find you anything you need."

"Thank you kindly," Ofelia said.

As Ofelia browsed the collection, nothing in particular stood out to her. She needed something special, that could help her pass the time during the long days and nights that she was alone. Ofelia felt a little disappointed that nothing stood out to her that morning. After a few hours, she was about to give up her search until she gazed over and saw a cart filled with books. The books were not just any books, they were damaged books.

"May I look over here?" she asked the librarian.

"Those books are going into the trash," she said. Ofelia looked at her in disbelief.

"May I look at them before you dispose of them please?"

"I suppose so."

Ofelia walked over and looked through every book on the cart. To her surprise, there were a lot of great books on the cart. Surely the books could be salvaged, she thought. She thought about the bird with the bad wing, who visited her that summer in the fields. He didn't look like the other birds, he was a little slow to start but once he flew, he soared like the others. If the bird could fly, and I could learn to read, how much more could the books be brought back to life, she thought. She asked the librarian if she could help her restore the books and like, most other people Ofelia presented an idea to, the lady could not refuse.

"If we are going to do this, then we should get started immediately, before I change my mind!"

The two of them spent the next couple of days restoring the books and making them shine again. The old damaged books on the cart turned out to be some literary classics. Ofelia shared her story with the librarian about the journey she was on. The librarian was intrigued by Ofelia and thought she was the bravest woman she had ever met. After the two of them restored the books, Ofelia decided it was time to move on to the next destination.

"Please take as many of the books as you want," the librarian told her. She certainly wanted some of the books, but she knew that she wouldn't be able to carry much of anything else in her bag.

"How about this, I can leave some of my books here and take a few," Ofelia compromisingly suggested.

The librarian thought it was a great idea. Ofelia grabbed five books from her bag, in exchange for three from the collection. She purposefully chose the most damaged books, the ones that still had marks and a few torn pages in them; she loved their character.

"You want those ones?" the librarian asked.

"Yes, I'll take the most damaged books, to serve as a reminder of this valuable experience."

"Okay, you should do what you feel you ought to do. I appreciate you helping me restore the books and I wish you love and light on your continued journey."

Ofelia was delighted and proud of the work that was accomplished. That night she wrote, *Sometimes, strangers are placed in our path to help reaffirm the things we know to be true.* Ofelia was glad to be moving on to the next destination, she felt the experience she had at the library, was the reason for her passing through the town.

She hopped on the moving train, with more ease than before. As the wind blew through her hair, she felt increasingly empowered, as if the world was putty in her hands. There would be nothing she couldn't do. As she arrived at the next town, she was relieved that it was still light outside. She wanted to get started on her next experience as soon as possible. During her stay in the new- found town, she would need to work, as her money was quickly diminishing. She ate fruit from the fields whenever she could, but she needed more substance at times and food was not cheap. She knew she would have to stay in town for a little while, to save money for the next adventure. She wanted to try something new besides picking fruit and vegetables in the fields, the only work she had previously known.

Ofelia wandered around town, relieved that it felt cozier and friendlier than the last. Everyone greeted her, as if she belonged there. Maybe there were a lot of transplants in the town, she thought. It looked like it was being developed and larger than the last town. People seemed more open-minded and Ofelia appreciated that. One day she sat in the park, reading the books she had taken from the library, occasionally standing up to stretch her legs. She decided to walk over to the playground for a change of scenery. She sat on the park bench and watched the children play, she enjoyed watching their innocence, seeing their smiles, and carefree spirits. She knew that someday, she would have children of her own and would get to watch them play. She imagined sitting on a park bench, wondering what dreams they would have for their own lives.

"Are you caring for children here?" a woman sitting on the next bench asked.

"No ma'am," she answered.

"Oh, I'm sorry, I thought you were a nanny."

"No ma'am, I just arrived into town, I am not working yet."

"Well, I am looking for a nanny, perhaps you would be interested in caring for my two boys," the woman said as she wrote down her address on a scrap piece of paper and handed it to Ofelia.

"Thank you kindly, ma'am, I will come by tomorrow morning to speak to you."

Ofelia had never taken care of children, as she was the baby of the family. Although she had nieces and nephews, she had never solely been responsible for any of them. She wasn't confident that she was qualified, but nonetheless needed a job. It wouldn't hurt to go and speak to the woman, she thought. The next morning, she got up bright and early and headed to the address that the woman provided. It took Ofelia a while to find the house but once she did, she was in absolute splendor at the site of it. She thought that perhaps, someday, she could own a magnificent house herself. The grass was the greenest grass she had ever seen, and the white picket fence made it picturesque. Ofelia had visualized such houses and saw some in books but had never actually seen one in person. As she passed the front gate, she was immediately greeted by the woman from the park.

"Hello," my name is Susan, the lady enthusiastically said, with her hand stretched out.

"It is nice to formally meet you Susan, I'm Ofelia."

She then invited Ofelia back to the yard to meet the children. Susan had a table of food set out on the porch and Ofelia was anxious to taste every single treat. Susan had two boys, twins, Michael and Matthew. They were three years old and quite the handful from what Ofelia could see thus far. "Cute kids, Susan," Ofelia sincerely said. The boys looked exactly the same, Ofelia wondered how they could be told apart. Ofelia kneeled down to her knees to greet the playful, mischievous, toddlers. The boys both took to her almost instantly. She grabbed their hands and played ring around the rosy with them and they laughed each time they fell on their bottoms; she made them smile. Susan was excited to see the instant connection that Ofelia had with the boys. Susan explained that the boys had gone through a couple of nannies, and that she was well aware that they were a lot of work.

"I need a nanny during the week, while I help my husband at the hardware store. We also like to entertain during the weekends and we would expect you to be available during those times as well."

Ofelia listened to the expectations and figured she really didn't have anything going on at that moment, so why not accept the offer? "Also, we would like for you to live onsite, you can stay in the treehouse that we built for the boys." Ofelia looked beyond to see the house sitting atop of the tree. The treehouse looked charming and was certainly an upgrade to the old train accommodations; the offer was one that Ofelia couldn't pass up.

"I would be honored to work for you Susan, and the treehouse looks enchanting, when should I start?"

"You can begin right now."

Ofelia felt relieved that she would have somewhere safe to sleep that night; the treehouse ended up being a real bonus. And as it turned out, Susan's husband was quite the carpenter, the treehouse was more of a mother-in-law house, it had everything Ofelia needed. *It's amazing how the things you need the most, fall right into your hands, when you need them to,* Ofelia wrote in her journal. That night as she closed her eyes, she believed that her sister must have been thinking of her and wishing her the best and that's why she was presented with the unexpected blessing.

Ofelia spent the next couple of years living in the treehouse, helping to raise the twins. She also took on more responsibilities as the housekeeper and the cook; she did everything for the family and was appreciated and well compensated for her hard work. Susan knew that she loved books and bought Ofelia more than she could read in a lifetime. The books were stacked high in the treehouse. Ofelia did some of her best writing within the walls of the treehouse, it was a magical place. Overall, she was grateful for the years that she had spent with the family. She learned how to care for little ones, which grew her patience and during that time, she had become quite domesticated. She knew that when she was blessed with children of her own someday, that she would be more than ready. *Much of what we learn is by actually doing, I know what kind of mother I will be,* she wrote. *The kind of mother who rocks my children to bed at night, reads them a good story, and builds them up to believe that they can be anything.* Ofelia had many deep and sometimes random thoughts. She recorded a lot of things, so that she would not forget what she was learning along her journey.

Ofelia wanted to get back home eventually, but not until she was ready. She wasn't sure exactly when that would be. She missed everyone and not a day went by that she didn't think about her beloved family. She stayed in contact through occasional letters. *Many of life's journey's must be traveled alone,* she wrote. She learned a lot about timing and trusting herself. She would know the day that she should return home to visit, and she knew that her family would welcome her with arms wide open. *Mami and Papi ask for you all the time Paloma, and I tell them that you are living your dreams and they say they are proud of you,* Lourdes wrote in a letter.

Ofelia was content but growing a little stagnant with the life that she was in. She felt that it was time to move on, to do more exploring. She felt she had learned all that she could, and it was time to grow. She was now twenty-one and had blossomed into a more confident, eloquent young woman. She thought about when she had left home, she was just a foolish young girl, in search for deeper things in life, she realized how naïve she was. The time she spent with the family taught her how to be responsible and she was grateful for that. She knew that when she moved on to another destination, that she would somehow have to merge the carefree soul she was, with the new responsible, more sensible, woman that she had become.

"Susan, thank you so much for sharing your family with me. You have all made me feel a part of your family and I have learned greatly from the experience; it was an honor to work for you."

Susan was saddened to see Ofelia go but she had grown to love her so much that she supported her decision.

As Ofelia headed out of town, she was better equipped for the journey. She had saved money and was now able to purchase a ticket, on a passenger train. As the conductor gave a last call, Ofelia couldn't have been more excited. The one-way ticket she purchased was to Denver, Colorado. She had read about the beauty of the Rocky Mountains and longed to see them for herself. As she arrived in Denver, with a suitcase in tow, she could feel the cold on her face that reassured her that she was alive and well. In fact, she had never felt more alive than she had in that moment. She had grown in knowledge, matured through experience, and she anticipated something great. She anticipated something life changing, even greater than before. Ofelia stepped off the train, dressed as if she were going somewhere important, perhaps she had a predestined date with fate. She knew she wouldn't be disappointed because she had learned to trust herself.

She had enough money to get a place to stay right away. She quickly made friends and soon loved living in Denver. It was a bigger city than anywhere she had previously been. She learned to drive and was working at a local restaurant. She decided the job would be temporary, until she could figure out where her passion lied. She took the job in stride and met a lot of different people that she learned a great deal from. She loved spending time with her friends and was a joy to be around. Her girlfriends felt inspired by her zeal for life and her ambitious nature. She shared so much of what she had learned with others, she had become wise beyond her years.

Each Friday morning as Ofelia opened the restaurant, she would see a young handsome man in the parking lot across the street working on an old Chevy truck. She could see how he would get frustrated at times but continued to work on the truck, he was there at the same time every Friday morning. She started to look forward to watching him through the window. She wanted to know more about him, like who he was. Surely, he must have had a story, she thought. Her curiosity was greater than herself and she decided she would go over to say hello the following Friday.

As she drew the shades open to the large window at the restaurant, he glared over at her with the biggest brown eyes she had ever seen. He was tall and slender and had a very distinctive walk; a walk of unexplainable confidence. She became a bit intimidated and reconsidered her introduction. Just as she decided she wouldn't cross the street, the young man started across the street, straight toward her. She got nervous and quickly withdrew the window shade, hoping that he hadn't seen her. Since the door was already opened, the young man could freely walk in, and so he confidently did. As he entered the restaurant, she grabbed a coffee cup and acted like she was polishing the outer rim.

"I wondered how many more Friday mornings you were going to watch me," the young man said.

"I don't know what you're talking about," she shyly said.

She was filled with embarrassment and felt ever so foolish. Then it occurred to her that he must have been equally watching her.

In a sarcastic tone, she then asked, "Well, if you saw me watching you week after week, why didn't *you* come over to speak to me?"

The young man could see that she had a spunky personality, and he liked it.

"I suppose a proper introduction is in order," he said. "My name is Leo Ramos."

The two offered each other their hands and once their hands met, they held on longer than a brief, formal handshake. Every Friday after that, Leo came by the restaurant to greet Ofelia. She had read so many love stories and thought that perhaps she had met the man, that would be the main character in her own love story. She was patient and allowed for love to blossom in its own season. A season of love would surely come upon her, she was convinced of it.

Leo was the most handsome man she had ever laid eyes on. She loved the way he smiled, the way he spoke, and especially his scent. She could smell him even when he wasn't present. He was a perfect vision of a strong man and they had similar backgrounds that made her feel comfortable around him. He was also from northern California and too had recently relocated to Denver. Ofelia definitely knew how to keep his attention. Sometimes she talked very fast, as she had so much to say and at times he could barely keep up, but oddly enjoyed the challenge. He really learned to care for her; he was very sweet and wanted to give her everything she deserved in life. He supported her dreams and never doubted her in anything. He was completely confident in her abilities and wanted her to feel like she could truly be herself around him. *Be with someone who supports your dreams and allows you to be yourself*, she wrote in a journal she entitled *Love Blossoms*. The journal held everything she had ever learned about love between a man and a woman. *Sometimes love is a beautiful mess*, she wrote.

Ofelia loved being in love and since the first day she and Leo had met, she remained in love every day that followed. Ofelia felt that Leo was her soulmate, she trusted herself and allowed love to completely enter in, as Leo did that morning at the restaurant. Soon she and Leo were on to something beautiful; the greatest love either of them had ever known. They spent day after day learning how to make one another happy. *I live every day to make this man smile*, she wrote. As the two of them grew closer she learned everything about him. She respected him and admired how he showed love and generosity to everyone. He was the most caring man she had ever met; he loved passionately and unconditionally. She learned a great deal from him and he undoubtedly made her a better person. His love was infectious, and she never felt so complete. She wondered what was next; even though she was uncertain as to the details, she knew that she had found her life partner.

A year after Leo walked into the restaurant, is when their love story would truly begin. Ofelia loved spending every free moment she had with Leo. Sometimes he would come to visit with her while she was working. He knew how much she loved to socialize with the customers and he was there to see her smile. They were a popular couple around the neighborhood. They were a power couple who could also shine on their own. Leo was a romantic and being the giving soul that he was, he regularly showered Ofelia with gifts; simple, thoughtful gifts and she appreciated the gestures. During that time, it was customary for men to be macho, but Leo treated Ofelia as an equal and she would have it no other way. She was much too strong willed to allow anyone to dim her colorful personality. Ofelia started to feel like she should take Leo to meet her family back home. Since she hadn't been back for a few years, she decided that the visit was overdue. She realized that her parents were getting older and she truly missed them, Lourdes, and the rest of the family.

"Leo, do you want to go with me back home to visit my family?"

"Of course, Ofelia, you know I would travel to the moon and back with you."

Since he loved to see her smile, he would do just about anything to keep a smile on her face. Little did she know, that Leo had been waiting for the opportunity to meet her family. He felt the timing was right, as they had met exactly a year earlier.

And so, the couple packed up Leo's blue Chevy and headed to California. It was a long drive, that took them nearly two days but the laughs and conversation they had during the drive made the time pass effortlessly. "I don't know what I would do without you, Leo, my best friend, you have brought an unexplainable love into my life, I have never known a love like this." Ofelia was committed to Leo and he was equally committed. They were young, but they wouldn't allow age to prevent them from planning a future together. Ofelia wanted Leo by her side, on every adventure, going forward. "I am so thrilled that I finally get to see my family!" she said.

Leo could hear the excitement in her voice. He was honored to be a part of the reunion. He knew everything about her family; Ofelia talked about them a lot. It was as if they all still played a vital role in her everyday life, although they were not there in the flesh. Leo was a good listener, he remembered everyone's name and the little details about each of their personalities. He bought a special edition knife from the army surplus, to take as a gift for Ofelia's father; he remembered that her father was a knife collector.

Ofelia's family anxiously awaited their arrival. As the blue truck drove up to the driveway, Ofelia could see Lourdes and her mother sitting on the old beat up rocking chairs, that sat in the front of the house since she was a child. As soon as Lourdes spotted the truck, she jumped up out of the chair, nearly tripping over it, to get close to her sister. Ofelia could see her mother, moving significantly slower than Lourdes, getting out of the other beat up chair. Lourdes ran down the long drive way and Ofelia had an instant flash back of her older sister running through the sunflowers holding her tiny hand, as they headed to the school house. Ofelia's heart was overflowing with joy and for a moment she wondered why she had waited so long to be reunited with her family. As she shook off the thought, she knew there must have been a reason she hadn't felt it was the right time to return, until then. Leo could barely stop the truck when Ofelia jumped out, mid motion; she could not contain her excitement. "Ofelia, hold on!" he shouted. He slammed on the brakes, but she had already flown out, like a free bird.

"Paloma!"

"Lourdes, my beloved sister!"

The embrace they shared was like a rejoining of one heart; they were overjoyed. Lourdes touched Ofelia's face, as if she was making sure she was real. "Mami!" Ofelia greeted her mother with a hug and a kiss on the cheek. Her mother held her for a few seconds and then said, "Let's go inside, in Spanish." Just as the three of them were about to enter the house, Ofelia remembered Leo was still in the car. "Come on Leo!" she excitedly said as she motioned him over. As Leo exited the truck, both Lourdes and their mother greeted him with a hug.

"We have heard so much about you Leo," Lourdes said. Every letter Lourdes got from Ofelia describing him was poetic. She knew without a doubt that her sister had found her soul mate and she shared in her joy. It was almost instant that Leo was accepted by the family.

As they finally entered the house, they could see that the entire family was there. Ofelia was overwhelmed, as it was her first-time meeting some of the younger children and babies. Everyone was thrilled to see her and relieved that she appeared safe and sound. Ofelia had shocked everyone with the way she abruptly left; many of them were concerned for her safety because she was just a young lady.

They could see that Ofelia had certainly grown into a woman; a poised woman with a joyful smile. A few family members expressed that her leaving was probably the best thing she could have done, although her departure was hard on them. *You cannot subdue a free bird*, Ofelia wrote in one of her many journals. Ofelia tried to ease her family's minds by staying in touch through occasional letters. Most of them agreed that receiving a letter here or there, was better than no contact at all. Leo felt honored that Ofelia deemed him worthy enough, not only to meet her family, but to be present at the special reunion.

The house was filled with a completeness that day, the last piece to the puzzle had been found. Ofelia almost forgot what it felt like to be a part of a family. *There is nothing like the love amongst family,* she wrote. Ofelia's father was expected to arrive at any time and Ofelia couldn't wait to see him; Leo was a little nervous though. He remembered the stories that Ofelia told him about her father and he knew that he wouldn't approve of just anyone, not for his daughter. And although Ofelia had been traveling solo for some time, Leo knew that her father's protective nature would soon be displayed. "Grand Papa is here!" one of the smaller boys enthusiastically yelled. As Ofelia's father entered the house filled with love, he ran towards Ofelia and picked her up, as if she was a small child again. Memories of her father briefly ran through her mind and she then realized that she hadn't appreciated him enough for the man that he truly was. He was a man of very few words but that particular day he said, "This is a glorious day, as my Paloma has returned, we celebrate the return of our wondrous one"! She was shocked that he had learned to speak better English since she left, she was proud of him and he was equally as proud of her.

The family joined in a celebratory evening, filled with food and dancing. Everyone wanted to hear about where Ofelia had been; she had several side conversations with various family members throughout the night. Everyone admired her brave heart and were in awe of her strong will to explore different places. Everyone was very welcoming towards Leo and he felt comfortable around her family. The evening came to a beautiful end and Ofelia thanked Leo for taking her to see her family. "It has been an honor to witness the unconditional love that your family has for you," he said. Ofelia and Leo planned to stay and visit for a few days.

Ofelia went to sleep that night believing that she was where she needed to be, and she closed her eyes with a heart of gratitude. It turned out that Leo had a plan of his own and was awaiting the perfect time to execute his plan.

The following day, the men of the family invited him to join them out to the porch to have some drinks and a cigar, he gladly accepted the invitation. The men talked shop and Leo fit in well with them. After a while, Ofelia's father and Leo had an opportunity to talk one on one; their conversation went on for hours. It didn't hurt that Leo was fluent in Spanish; the two of them met in the middle, conversing both in English and Spanish. Ofelia's father could tell that Leo was a man of strong character, in actually the two of them were very similar. Leo couldn't end the night without asking the burning question.

"Señor, may I have your blessing to ask Ofelia for her hand in marriage?"

"I thank you for having the respect to formally ask me for my daughter's hand, but the reality is, Ofelia has left the nest years ago, and therefore is free to decide whom she will marry."

"Señor, I understand that your daughter is *unique*."

"Ofelia has always had her own thoughts, her own visions and a curiosity that cannot be contained." "Are you willing to journey with her?" her father cautiously asked.

"Yes, Señor, I will journey with her to the ends of the earth and anywhere else that her heart desires, I assure you that she was created for me and me for her. I will live everyday ensuring that her soul is the happiest on earth."

Her father was impressed with him and could see the genuine love he had for his daughter. Her father was pleased that Ofelia had chosen such a great man.

"You two are welcome to marry here in our backyard if you wish."

"Thank you, Señor, if that's what Ofelia wants, that is what we will do."

Leo and Ofelia were joined in matrimony by the end of the week. Ofelia chose not to wear a traditional dress, instead, she wore a long, flowy, canary colored dress with baby breath placed throughout her long wavy hair. Leo thought she was a vision of that of a delicate rose. The two joined hearts on that glorious day with the blessings of every present soul. The love they shared could be felt by everyone at the union. It was a perfect day and Ofelia thanked the universe for sending her a journey partner. Since she had him, she knew that she would never be alone again. After the vows were spoken, the two love birds danced like never before, they danced to the beat of their own hearts, anyone could see that their love was perfection.

Ofelia and Leo stayed in town for a couple of more weeks but had to get back soon as Leo was starting a new job in Denver. As they packed up, Ofelia's parents and Lourdes were standing outside on the front porch, waiting for them. Ofelia was sad to say good bye again, but she was also equally as excited for her future. "I love you Mami, Papi and my sister, I will do my best to make all of you proud of the life I create," Ofelia said. "We are already proud of you daughter," her father said as he choked up and closed the door to the blue Chevy. As Leo put the truck into drive, Ofelia stuck her head out and waved her arm from out of the window. As they left a trail of dust behind, her family knew that she would be better than okay.

As Leo and Ofelia got settled into their adult lives, they learned even more about each other. Ofelia was a great wife and

Leo appreciated her devotion to the marriage. He was a sound provider and made her feel secure by not disappointing her. They both wanted children and they planned on having at least four or five. They began growing their family almost immediately and were wonderful parents, who lived for their children. *I never knew that being a mother would be this rewarding*, she wrote in her journal. Leo was not only a solid provider but he equally spent time with the children, giving each of them individual attention.

He wasn't like a lot of the other fathers in the neighborhood, who believed that their only job was to work to put food on the table, Leo refused to be that kind of dad. He didn't have a very good relationship with his own father growing up and he refused to be anything like him. Leo's parent involvement was a positive example for a lot of the other dads around the neighborhood. He mentored some of the men, motivating them to be more involved in their children's lives. Ofelia and Leo were admired by so many. They began to be engaged around the community, by helping neighbors register to vote, and leading union efforts for underpaid workers. They were well respected and loved helping others whenever they could. Their four children Hector, Martha, Marisol and Juanito, were all very intelligent and well behaved. Leo and Ofelia often talked about the dreams they had for each of them individually. They considered it a blessing to parent such bright children. *The universe has entrusted us with four souls, and we will inspire them to change the world by our example,* Ofelia wrote.

One starry night while Ofelia and Leo were returning from their weekly date night, they talked about how much they loved each other, as if they were still newlyweds. They recalled sharing an ice cream cone from the parlor down the street. He liked chocolate and she liked vanilla, so they would share a twist cone.

"This is how love should feel all the time," she told Leo as she looked him in the eyes. "I promise to never let this feeling fade, I love you more and more every day."

"You, my love, you have been all I expected and more, I thank my lucky stars for you every night," he responded.

Ofelia scooted over to the driver's side of the old blue Chevy and put her arm around her man. As they pulled up to the house they could see smoke coming from the windows. Leo quickly parked the truck and jumped out; he ran as fast as his long legs could move. He could see the neighbors gathered around and immediately counted three small heads. "Where's Juanito?" he shouted. The other kids were hysterical and could barely speak. Leo decided not to wait for an answer, as it would probably not be the answer he wanted to hear. He immediately ran to the back of the house, which seemed to be less aflame. "Leo, no!" Ofelia screamed. But before she could stop him, a neighbor, *Sully Gutiérrez*, ran from across the street with baby Juanito in his arms. Ofelia frantically grabbed her son and ran to the back of the house to tell Leo that Juanito was safe. She waited and waited, but Leo never came out of the house. She felt helpless, as she watched the flames engulf the house.

That night, Ofelia lost her eternal love and she knew she would never be the same again. She would never love again; her heart was made for him. She couldn't help feeling angry at him for leaving her. But she also understood that he ran into the flames to save their son. She didn't know how she would raise four children, by herself. She didn't believe it possible to play both roles. *Life can be unfair, and I hope to fully understand the reason for this terrible event, someday*, she wrote.

It took a lot of strength and faith for Ofelia to go on. She was challenged like never before and many of nights she cried for her lost love, her journey partner. Lourdes moved to Denver to help Ofelia with the children, and she was forever indebted to her. Ofelia began working soon after Leo's passing. Family and friends helped with money and groceries, in which she was grateful for, but she ultimately knew that she had to provide for her children, on her own. Being a widower was a role that Ofelia never fathomed she would assume. The night of the fire changed the whole narrative of her life. Raising two young men was also very challenging for a single woman, she did the best she could under the circumstances.

"I am proud of the mother you have become Ofelia," Lourdes said.

"I couldn't do this without you," Ofelia replied.

Ofelia was grateful that her sister sacrificed so much to come and help her with the children. Ofelia's parents gifted her with enough money to help rebuild the family home, the tiny yellow house on Sherman Street. Soon after the fire and house rebuild, Ofelia got a job, in fact, she got two jobs. One job was cleaning at a hotel during the day, and the other was waitressing in a restaurant at night. She felt sad for not spending as much time as she would've liked to, with the children, but she had no other choice.

Her day began at three o'clock in the morning. She would make sack lunches for the children, enclosing notes inside to re-affirm her love for them. She assembled the sack lunches while dinner was cooking. She felt a responsibility to make sure the children had a homemade meal every night and Lourdes assured her that she would have them sit and enjoy dinner together.

Ofelia worked hard, and exhaustion became a normal state for her. Her only escape from her reality was reading and writing, and she did so anytime she had a break at either job. She believed that some of her most heartfelt writing was done during those most difficult years. Ofelia would stare out of the restaurant window, wondering where the birds were going, just as she did as a young girl. Some days she wanted to fly away too. She felt like a bad mother for wanting to escape; she knew that she would never leave her children, but her mind and heart were severely damaged. She tried to be happy for the children and often times hid her true feelings from everyone. Ofelia put forth her remaining energy into transforming her mind to travel to other places, places that made her heart happy. She knew that someday, she would share her true life with her family in the hopes that they would gain a better understanding of who she was and who she wanted to be.

She wrote: *Life can be anything you want it to be, based on how deeply you want to dream. Someday you will understand why I've lived a series of lifetimes, through my journeys, and since I have not been able to accomplish these things in the physical realm, I urge you all to make your experiences a true reality. On my last day here on earth, I will be content with the world of fantasy that I had created for myself, it was the best I could do with what I was given. I hope that you will find me to be strong and wise, in these books you will find tools you need to live out your individual dreams. I have thought about each one of you, and that's why I have used these books to inspire you. Whether or not you utilize these ingredients to enhance your lives, just know that my intention is to prompt you to live your best life. May I always be someone you look up to, for the simple fact that I considered you in everything I've done.*

I don't believe that the stories I've shared are a fallacy because, in my mind and in my heart, I was really there. I always knew I was destined for something bigger than myself and now I know that my purpose was to leave you with this hope. You need to believe that you can be anything, do anything, do more than one thing, and be more than one person. It's ok to have dreams and it's okay not to always know the right thing to do, life will only be mastered when you see what others have done with the legacy you left. Even though, I may not have climbed a volcano or talked to birds, I've played it all out, so you could believe in the impossible. Some things will never be seen with natural eyes, only felt with the heart. You all have different gifts and possibilities; do not sit by the wayside and watch others take their place in the world. **Do Something,** *do something good, something noble. It is now your turn to build a legacy for your children, therefore make your story a good one.*

The time was drawing close; Ofelia knew her spirit would be leaving her body soon. She grabbed her gold locket from around her neck. And with barely enough strength, she opened it up. As her tiny, old, rough hands unlatched it, she smiled at the old black and white picture of her tall standing husband, Leo. She could see them dancing together under the stars and her laughing aloud at his corny jokes. She looked over at the empty chair beside the bed, and there sat her beloved. Leo looked exactly as he had the day they met, when he came into the restaurant, she could smell him. She wasn't frightened, she felt an overwhelming comfort like she had when they were together.

"My beloved Leo," she said with a gracious smile.

"It's time to fly Ofelia," he said.

"I know the story is about to end," she said.

"No, my dear, the story is just beginning. You see Ofelia, that day in the fire as I entered the burning house, I had a unique experience; I have waited a lifetime to share it with you." Ofelia looked at him and with a slight nod, prompted him to tell her of the details.

"As I entered the burning house searching for Juanito, there were flames all around me. I could see butterflies flying around the house, *unharmed*. The flames were strong and overwhelming me and as I fell to the ground, engulfed with fire, I heard a voice. The voice asked me to make a choice." Her curiosity grew expeditiously at what he was explaining.

"I was given the choice to live or die, based on my love for you. If I chose to live that day, your mind would not have been able to venture in the way it has all these years. I knew that the life you always wanted would not have been possible with me in it, and I had to allow you to dream."

"I was told that if I chose to die, in order to give you, life, that we would have eternity together, so I chose death. You see in the end I loved you so much that I was willing to sacrifice a temporary life with you. I knew that you were called to a high purpose; I was simply placed in your path to lead you to that purpose. I watched you teach our children and grandchildren, in only the way you could, and I was watching you every step of the way."

"And so ultimately, I gave my life for you so that you could make your life the best story ever told. You see, we both win in this journey, you lived your best life and now I have you for eternity, my love. And this is why our children, our grandchildren and their children, will be able to call you, the most magnificent woman they have ever known."

And just like that, Nana Ofelia and Grandfather Leo entered into eternity. The two birds soared high above the clouds and pursued a new journey together. Whether or not this depiction of such a magnificent woman is truth or fallacy, we may never know. I have simply interwoven pieces of fabric that she left for the world to learn from. But one thing I am certain of, is her intent to inspire others to live a full life; a life filled with wonder and adventure.